THE DEMON KING'S PET

ERI EVERLAND

NOTE

Eri Everland is rebranding her author pen name as of 2026. Depending on when you read this, you may seem some title reflect the former name, Ever Eri.

CONTENT WARNING

The content in this book may not be suitable for everyone. Please be aware that this book contains the following:

Explicit sex scenes
Tail Play
Violence

To the beauties who have ever been made to feel like you're not good enough because of your size, you deserve to be loved. You deserve to be happy.

You are *enough.*

Chapter 1

I plucked a fanged beetle off the green tomatoes. It'd be a few weeks before they turned that beautiful deep red that indicated they were ready to eat, and I wasn't about to let a fruit-sucking insect destroy my hard work. Soon my family could indulge in a spring treat if I protected them long enough to ripen. Dark gray clouds hovered in the distance, threatening a late winter storm that could destroy all my hard work. I had watched them all morning, praying to the gods and goddesses that the storm would continue on, passing by Narthington, my small town.

It had been months since my family had the delight of fruit. We couldn't afford the ones merchants sold in the winter months, imported from the warm southern territories. In the summer, we could spare a few coins for fresh produce, but I wanted to do something to help my family, since I wasn't useful like my brother. I couldn't bring home funds like he did from physical labor. The most I could do was help within the home by mending ripped clothing, helping my mother cook, and taking care of my baby sister when others were preoccupied. And my garden. It was the one thing that was uniquely mine.

I dreamed of having a large garden with flowers and fruits from across the continent. It'd be a place where everyone would come to admire my hard work and realize gardening was so much more than playing in the dirt. If I could ever get my hands on a bleeding heart lily, my dream would be complete.

I knew that dream was nothing more than fantasy. I would have to marry rich to have enough coin to build a garden like that—something only pretty girls could manage.

The silver windmills turned as the wind changed direction, shifting the storm directly towards my garden. I'd have to cover the delicate plants with my worn tarp and hope it was enough to stave off the frost that threatened the temperamental leaves.

"Nyri!" My mother's lilting voice echoed from inside. "Nyri! Where are you?"

"I'm outside, mother!" I would have to come back to cover my garden later. I had a few hours before the storm would make it to town, and there was a chance it would change directions yet again.

"Nyri! Hurry." My father's booming voice was like the drum to my mother's music, steady and unwavering.

I brushed the dirt off my pants, wishing I had time to change before facing my parents, but their calls sounded urgent. Making them wait was worse than the looks they'd give me once they found out I was in my garden again. I dipped my hands in the bucket of water by the door, ignoring the freezing temperature. It was early spring, but the weather belonged to the winter months.

My parents were waiting in the family room, and my mother held Melody, my baby sister, in her arms. Even my younger brother was there. Five years my junior, Harlan was twenty years old. He was young and strong, making him desired by the farmers in town. He brought home as much gold as my father on a bad week.

My mother's nose wrinkled as she studied the stains on my pants. "Were you playing in your dirt again? No wonder none of the boys in town wish to marry you."

Her insult reflected off my steel chest. After spending my life dealing with slander from not only the townsfolk but also my family, I had grown used to their harsh words. I wondered if there'd be a day when my family's opinion stopped bothering me.

"Now, now, that's not the reason they don't want her," my father chimed in. I hoped he was about to defend me, but I should've known better. "If she was pretty, Nyri could get away with her strange hobbies, but boys don't like girls with rolls on their bodies."

"It wouldn't hurt to wear a skirt occasionally. It'd hide that fat on your belly. Oh, and if you curled your hair, others wouldn't notice the plain, brown nature of it," my mother chirped.

I curled my fingers into fists to stop myself from running my fingers over my curves and messing with my hair. I was the only one who had a weight issue in my family, and they never let me forget it. They never let me forget everything they found wrong with my looks.

"The tomatoes will be ready in a few weeks. I wanted to check on them, since it looks like a storm might be coming." It was best not to argue with my family's snide remarks. It only made me feel worse. They loved me. They just didn't know how to express it properly.

"The Ballion family had me there extra early to prepare for a frost that could ruin crops," Harlan said. My brother never directly defended me from my parents, but he tried in his own subtle way.

"Now, that's real work." My father was a large, muscular man, and he had barely slowed down as I got older. He prided himself on hard work and admired others who did the same, but his definition of hard work didn't include women who liked to garden.

I cleared my throat, knowing I wasn't called into the family room to discuss the frost. "Did you need something?" I was eager to get back to my garden. After a long winter, I was ready for food that wasn't dried meat and nuts.

My mother stopped herself mid-sentence to respond. "Yes, that's right. Your father and I have been talking, and we think it's time for you to move out of the house."

I laughed. It had to be a joke. When no one else joined in, my body went numb. My mother and father stared at me with unflinching faces. Harlan avoided my eyes. I swallowed hard, trying to get a grasp on my shock. "What do you mean? I can't leave."

My father crossed his arms. "You do not contribute enough to this household, and it's clear that you will not find a match for marriage, since you are past your prime. We cannot afford to continue feeding you. You will need to leave before nightfall."

I blinked several times. It had to be a bad dream. My family loved me. "And where shall I go?" I waited for them to tell me it was a jest, some bad joke they had concocted from winter boredom.

My mother clicked her tongue. "That isn't our problem any longer. You had your chance to seduce a man, and you chose to play in your dirt instead. I warned you we wouldn't support you forever. It's not our fault you didn't take it seriously."

My hands shook, and I was going to be sick. My mother had harassed me about finding a husband, but there hadn't been a proper warning that I'd be kicked out if I failed. It wasn't like I hadn't *tried* to find someone to marry me.

This wasn't real. It couldn't be. My family loved me. They wouldn't kick me out like that. "I have contributed to the table by growing food. I thought I was doing my part."

"Puny fruit a few times a year does not make up for what you gorge yourself with daily." My father's voice was dry and bored. "We can no longer afford to feed you, and since you have no prospects, it's time for you to leave. Without you around, we can focus on Melody and make sure she succeeds where you have failed."

I could hardly breathe. My family loved me. I knew they did deep down. "I have nowhere to go."

"That isn't our problem." My mother stood and shifted Melody onto her other hip. My baby sister was nearly three. If I left now, she wouldn't remember me.

I looked up, forcing the tears back. I couldn't cry. I couldn't show weakness. That only made things worse. "Give me more time. I will find a marriage match this summer. Please."

"Be out by sundown, and don't you dare take anything that doesn't belong to you." My father followed my mother out of the room. There was no room for discussion. Their minds were made up.

"I have nowhere to go," I whispered under my breath, my mind reeling. No one in town would take me in if my own family wouldn't support me.

"Go to Ethlow," Harlan said. I had nearly forgotten he was there.

I looked at my brother. He had become a fine young man. He'd find a wife without issue and have a happy family. He was a hard worker, and he cared deeply. Harlan loved me. That much I knew, but his suggestion made me blanch. "Ethlow? The demon king's estate?"

"I heard from a friend that anyone who goes to Ethlow is welcome. No one is ever turned away. At least you'd have a roof over your head." With his tight voice, there was no doubt that he knew what he was suggesting, but he was right. If I didn't want to end up as a beggar on the streets, Ethlow was my only choice.

"Haven't you heard the rumors that whoever sells their soul to Ethlow never leaves again?"

The demon king lorded over Kinzlea, one of the five kingdoms on the continent ruled by demons. Once a year, a man with horns showed up to our small town to collect taxes, and in return, we were protected from the dangers of the outside world. However, the rumors about the demon king were never ending.

He ate the babies of women who wronged him.

He hunted humans for fun.

He drank the blood of virgins for power.

His crown was made from the bones of his enemies.

"That's just a rumor," Harlan said. "People exaggerate when they're scared."

For good reasons. Humans were nothing compared to demons, which is why we never challenged their rule. It was safer that way.

My brother didn't make me feel better. "He's a demon. His powers could crush a human like me with the blink of an eye."

Harlan was silent. He knew what kind of fate was ahead of me, but there was nothing he could do. He wasn't the head of the house. He didn't have the final say. "I fought for you, you know."

The smile I forced held no joy. "I know."

That was it. My fate was sealed. In a couple of hours, I'd be forced to leave the house I had known my entire life. I had no choice but to make the journey to Ethlow, where I'd never see my family again.

"I'll come for you," Harlan said. He crossed the room and grabbed my hand. "When I save up enough to buy my own house, I *will* come for you."

I squeezed his hand, knowing it was the last time I'd see my brother. "Don't make promises you can't keep."

Harlan opened his mouth, but no words came out. He meant well, but by the time my brother made a home for himself, it'd be too late for me. I'd be living in the demon king's estate, tied to demons forever—unless I was already dead.

Chapter 2

My clothes were completely soaked, and my shoes squished with every step I took. The cold wasn't the worst part. My feet had gone numb from weeks of travel, and I walked with a limp after spraining my ankle on a rock in the middle of an unkempt path. I wanted to stop and rest, but I was afraid that if I stopped moving, I wouldn't be able to get back up.

The small bag I had packed had a single set of clothes to change into, rations that were long gone, a few coins Harlan had passed to me in secret, and seeds I hoped to use in a future garden.

The rain had stopped an hour ago, but mist lingered in the air, making it impossible for my clothes to dry. I could hardly see more than a few steps ahead of me, the fog hugging the ground closely. I wrapped my arms around my chest, but it did little to warm me. My bones had been chilled for days. I wanted to use the last of my coin for an inn, but I knew I needed it for food.

If I calculated correctly, I'd arrive at Ethlow before nightfall. The fog made it impossible to tell if I was on the right path. I couldn't track which way was north without the sun, so I pushed through the pain in my joints. One step after another.

I wondered if I had worked with Harlan more if my body wouldn't ache as much as it did. My mother constantly reminded me that the extra weight on my body hindered my daily life. If I was tired, it was because of the layer of fat over my muscles. It didn't matter how hard I had worked that day. I had no right to complain because my size was my fault.

I shifted my focus back to my feet. If I started feeling sorry for myself, I'd lose all motivation to keep going. One step after another.

I lost track of how long I had been walking, but when the path turned into an incline, I wanted to cry. I had never been in that much pain from walking before, but I had never walked that much all at once. My steps were slower, but as the path continued, the mist thinned. The sun broke through the clouds, and when I reached the top of the hill, the scenery was clear. I froze, staring at a large mansion made of black stone.

Ethlow.

The sun shone directly on the estate, but it looked like it was shrouded in darkness, as if it repelled the rays of the sun. A large, black gate surrounded a mansion, locking the unwanted out. Or keeping captives in. Bile crawled up my throat as fear washed over me. Everything about Ethlow looked dangerous. Knowing a demon king lived inside those lifeless stones only made my fear worse.

I wanted to turn around and run as far away from the castle as I could. I would die in that place if I stepped through those gates. I couldn't shake the feeling of death fluttering through my stomach.

I had nowhere else to go. My family had turned their backs on me, and I was all alone.

I took a step forward.

I'd die on the streets, alone, cold and broken.

Maybe death at the hands of a demon king would be more merciful.

Each step felt harder than the last, but I didn't dare stop. I wasn't sure I'd muster up the courage to start walking again if I stopped for a second. By the time I reached the iron gates, my entire body was numb—from fear or cold, I wasn't sure which. The gate creaked open when I pushed on it. It wasn't locked like I had expected.

Black stones led up to the front door, larger than any human needed, but I supposed what dwelled on the other side of the door wasn't human. Gold framed the door, making the black look darker. It was beautiful, but it didn't ebb my fear. My throat was dry, and my hand shook as I lifted it to the large, gold ring hanging from the mouth of a creature with a twisted face. The metal was warm against my hand, which surprised me. The chill in the air made my bones ache. The weather should've chilled a simple piece of metal, but the air buzzed with magic.

I knocked on the door three times before I lost courage. My hand slithered back to my side, and I held my breath as I waited for an answer.

Hardly any time passed as the door creaked open, seemingly on its own. I waited for someone to approach, but the doorway was empty. I leaned forward, poking my head through the opening while keeping my feet safe on the outside.

"Can I help you?"

I squeaked, jumping back as a tall figure slid out of the shadows in an unnaturally smooth manner. He wore a black blazer that was buttoned to the side with golden buttons. A dark teal shirt poked out from beneath the black. White gloves covered his hands, one of which rested on his stomach while the other was tucked behind him. He was tall, and as I looked up at his face, I lost my words. Horns that looked like the bones of bat wings poked from his head, and his eyes glowed an unnatural cyan color.

He wasn't human. His aura pulled the oxygen out of the air, making it suffocating as power pulsed through my veins. It was unlike anything I had experienced before, but I had never met a demon face-to-face. He looked down at me, waiting for a reply with unnatural stillness. It didn't look like he was breathing. He lifted his eyebrows. "Well?"

I willed myself to speak, but my throat was shut. My instincts told me to run. He was a predator, and I was the prey.

"Speak human, or leave."

My mouth gaped open, but I couldn't utter a single word.

The demon raised his eyebrows, waiting for me to say something. Anything. He would devour me whole if I couldn't speak, but I was convinced he would eat me even if I did say something.

"I don't have time for this." He stepped back inside and started shutting the door, shutting me out of the only place I had to go.

The only other option was to turn around and beg for someone in the nearest town to take me in—but that was unlikely.

"Work!" I felt simple the moment the word blurted from my mouth, but the door stopped moving.

The demon looked at me for a long moment. "Excuse me?"

"I can work for you." It was a miracle the words didn't come out as a stutter. "I have nowhere else to go, but I am a hard worker."

A closed-lip smile replaced his frown, but I imagined razor-sharp teeth hidden within. I was nothing compared to the power he held. I would be better off in the streets, but I had always imagined more for myself. I wasn't ready to let the world tear me down. Despite the fear, I knew this was where I needed to be if I wanted the chance to prove myself.

"She speaks," the demon said. He pushed the door open and motioned for me to step inside. My next test.

I took a deep breath and stepped over the threshold, the pain in my feet nothing compared to the fear in my heart. The mansion was warm, easily combating the chill of the lingering winter air. I wanted to cry as the heat caressed my skin, but the moment I was inside, the door slammed shut behind me, as if an invisible force decided I wasn't allowed to leave. I jumped and yelped, spinning around, but I came face-to-face with the demon. He had been behind me a moment ago, but he moved with impossible speed.

"Are you sure you're ready to take on the responsibility of a resident of Ethlow?" he asked, looming over me. He was tall—taller than anyone I had ever known before. It made me feel small, which was an incredible feat. My entire life had been filled with reminders of how big I was.

I nodded, unable to find my voice once again.

"Good. The first thing you need to know is that I am the master of the house. You can either call me 'Master' or 'Master Viridian.' If I hear you call me 'Viridian', you will be punished. If you have any issues while living here, you are to talk to me, not the king. Understood?"

"You're not the king?" With the power emanating from Viridian, I had been sure he was the demon king, ready to eat my soul.

"No. If you're lucky, you won't ever meet the demon king, which brings me to the rules of the house. There are only three rules, but if you wish to continue residing here, then you must follow them." Viridian paused for emphasis. He studied my every move, and despite knowing him for a few moments, it felt as if he could see into my soul and knew everything he needed to know about me.

"Rules. Got it. I can follow three rules." I looked away, unable to tame my erratic heart. I was convinced I'd end up as Viridian's dinner.

"Listen carefully because breaking the rules could result in your death. The first rule of the house is that everyone must do the work assigned to them. No one is allowed to live here for free. Everyone does their part, or they lose their residency. Do you have any useful skills?"

No. According to my mother, I wasn't useful, but I tried to tell myself that wasn't true. "I can patch holes in clothes, and—"

"Perfect. You will start as a seamstress first thing tomorrow morning. You will report to Malse."

There was no room to argue. If I had known he was going to take my first skill and assign me a job, I would've picked something else, but I didn't dare complain.

Viridian clasped his hands behind his back. "Rule number two: after sundown, you are not to step foot outside this house. During the day, if your work is done, you are free to roam the rest of the estate, but be inside before sundown." He didn't give an explanation as to why rule two was in place, but it was a miracle I hadn't passed out from fear. "Rule number three is the most essential rule. Never bother the demon king. If you find yourself in the same room as him, don't speak to him. Don't look at him. Leave the room immediately."

"Why?" I slammed my lips shut the moment the question slipped past my guard. I was in no position to ask questions.

Viridian's eyes flashed, a darkness spreading through him. Even if it wasn't a formal rule, it was clear that an unspoken rule was to never question the master of the house. His word was law. "If you agree to follow these three rules, I will show you where you will stay during your time here and give you a tour of the house. If you decline, I will show you the way out. So what is it?"

The way he ignored my question made two things clear. I wasn't going to learn about why I wasn't allowed to talk to the demon king, and I was insignificant to Viridian. Living in Ethlow was dangerous, but here, I'd have a roof over my head. If I kept my head down and followed the rules, maybe I could build a quiet life.

"I will follow your rules," I finally said, wondering if I was making the biggest mistake of my life.

"Follow me." It was the only form of acknowledgment I received from the demon before he walked past me.

My legs protested at the speed he moved, but I pushed myself to keep up with him. I didn't want to seem weaker than I already was. We passed the foyer and entered a grand hall. My pace slowed as I looked at the walls of books, paintings, and artifacts created from gold and jewels. One item alone could have fed my family for a year.

"Keep up," Viridian said with a click of his tongue.

I turned back to the master of the house, but my eyes fell on the landing hovering over the grand hall. A tall figure stood there grabbing the railing and looking directly at me. His yellow eyes glowed with an intensity that sent a shiver down my spine and moved directly between my legs. The power that flowed from him was nothing like Viridian's. It was strong but chaotic. It was unpredictable and all-consuming.

In an instant, I knew I was breaking rule three. I was staring at the demon king.

Chapter 3

Once my body hit my bed, I didn't move again until morning. Weeks of traveling and sleeping outside had exhausted me to a bone-deep level. My stomach woke me up, desperate after weeks of undereating. When I cracked my eyes open, I didn't remember where I was. For a moment, I wondered if it was all a bad dream.

My family loved me. They wouldn't kick me out.

The ceiling was made out of the same black stone that covered the outside of the building. It was like staring into an abyss. I stared into the darkness as my reality set in. This was my new home. I could die tomorrow, and no one would come looking for me. No one would miss me.

Maybe Harlan would remember me. Maybe he'd tell Melody the good memories of her older sister, so I wasn't completely erased from the outside world. Or maybe he'd get married, and I'd slowly fade from his life, becoming nothing more than a distant memory.

I forced myself to get out of bed, knowing feeling sorry for myself was a slippery slope. If I wasn't careful, I would end up staying in bed all day, and I would be kicked out of Ethlow, the one place a nobody like me could go. I didn't have any clean clothes to change into for my shift as a seamstress. After weeks of traveling, the one spare outfit I had packed was in worse condition than the clothes that clung to my body.

I slipped into the washroom connected directly to my room—something I couldn't comprehend. My family shared a single washroom, and no one got their own room. This was my space, according to Viridian. As long as I kept up with my share of the work in the household, I could stay until the day I died. It was a little difficult to believe. I could build a quiet life here. It wasn't what I had imagined, but it was better than being homeless.

I rinsed my clothes in an attempt to remove as much dirt as possible before hanging them up to dry while I slipped into the bathtub. The water poured from the spout, already warm. The estate was unlike anywhere I had stayed before. It ran with magic that was void in Narthington. It was strange and felt too luxurious for someone who had only a few coppers to her name.

After a bath that lasted too long, I slipped outside my room to search for food. The hallway was silent when I peeked my head out the door. The mansion was a maze, laced with stairs and hallways I struggled to comprehend. I had made a point to memorize the room I was to work in and the mess hall. Beyond that, the tour was a fading memory.

I hadn't met any of the other residents in my brief tour of the house. Only a few guards clad in dark leather armor had acknowledged my presence. It was as if everyone else knew to scatter at the sight of Viridian. A shiver ran down my spine at the thought of the demon. The less I dealt with him the better.

Despite the halls being empty, the mess hall buzzed with sounds. The moment I stepped inside, I froze, scanning the room, surprised by how many beings were scattered about, filling every table and the spaces in between. It wasn't just humans, either. There were beings with pointed ears, others with wings, some with both. One had light blue tinted skin, and another was as short as a young child with the face of a man in his fifties.

Narthington only had human residents. The towns I passed through to get to Ethlow were the same. I knew there were a plethora of races in the world, but I had lived a sheltered life, only running into a demon once before, and even that had been at a distance. My heart raced with fear and excitement as I looked at the room filled with lives from across the entire continent. Ethlow was the one place in Kinzlea where anyone could go if they had nowhere else to go.

No one bothered to look my way as I weaved between large and small bodies, making myself as small as possible. I was good at making myself invisible when it called for it. The fewer people who saw me, the fewer there were to notice my size in the first place. I snatched a round piece of bread and slipped back out of the hall. I nibbled on the food, not minding the plain taste. In the winter, it was rare for us to indulge in anything with proper seasonings until the summer months. I missed eating fruit, but I hoped to start a garden somewhere in Ethlow once I was settled.

I ate my small breakfast on my way to the sewing room, not wanting to be late on my first day. I had accidentally broken one of the three rules on my first day—thankfully I hadn't been caught—but I had no intention of breaking any more rules. I needed this place.

I stood in front of a wooden door, an image of a large needle and thread carved into the surface, making the identity of the room undeniable. I was unsure if I was supposed to knock or walk right in. My knuckles rapped against the door, deciding that was the polite option. I waited, wiping my fingers on my pants to remove any lingering crumbs. The door opened with a swiftness that made me jump. A woman stood on the other side. Her back was hunched, making her shorter than me by more than a full head. A scowl burned into her face, making the wrinkles around her lips and eyes seem deeper. Her ears came to a slight point, and her skin was tinted an olive-green color.

"Are you the new girl?" Her voice was deep and raspy.

I nodded, losing my voice.

She clicked her tongue as she looked me up and down. I curled my fingers into fists to stop them from shaking. She was either a troll or a goblin—I didn't know the difference, making me feel foolish and small. Either way, she looked sturdier than my human bones.

"You're late." She turned on her heels and snapped her fingers, walking away.

I followed behind her, the noise of the room filling my ears. There was no chatter, despite several bodies hunched over, working on various clothes. The clicking of machines echoed from a corner I couldn't see behind the piles of clothes and fabric nearly towering to the ceiling.

The woman stopped suddenly, and I barely stopped in time to avoid bumping into her. She snapped her fingers again. "Sit. You will work at this station. I was told you know how to sew." She didn't phrase it as a question, but she waited for an answer.

"I can do patchwork. I've never made anything from scratch."

"Today you will patch holes. Later you will learn to make clothes." She shoved a wooden box into my hands. "These are your tools. Do not lose them. You will have to pay to replace them."

"Do we get paid?"

Her frown lines deepened. "You will receive a stipend for the work you do as long as your work is sufficient."

I nodded, not daring to ask how much that stipend was. It didn't matter. Viridian said everything I needed would be provided during my stay as long as I did my share of the work. I hadn't asked for specifics. Earning a small stipend was more than I anticipated, but I could use it to purchase seeds and gardening supplies.

"Any other questions?" She stared at me with bulging eyes. It felt like a trick question, one that there was only one answer to.

"What's your name?"

A single blink. "Malse."

"I'm Nyri." I held my hand out to her.

She wrinkled her nose. "I don't care." She shoved a pile of clothes into my hands. "When you finish these. Find me." She left before I had a chance to ask her any other questions.

I sat down and sorted through everything to get a feel for my tools and the clothes I was handed. They were all male clothing, and the rips in the clothes weren't the kind I was used to. The holes didn't come from normal wear and tear. They were sliced all over. One by one, I patched the holes. For the most part, each piece of clothing only had a single tear. Halfway through the pile, there was one shirt that looked like someone had tried to shred it.

On the front of the shirt, there were four jagged rips. They looked like they were created from long claws, but I didn't know a beast like that. There were bears in Narthington, but they were docile creatures. One year, a pack of wolves had come too close to the farms and picked off a couple of the livestock. I had seen the injuries the hunters who faced the beasts had received, but they were nothing compared to the long scratches on the garment between my fingers.

I stood, my heart racing at the thought of something like that out there in the world. I knew the world outside Narthington was dangerous. I had heard plenty of stories, but that was all it was. *Stories.* I licked my lips, trying to bring moisture back to my mouth. I knew nothing about what had caused the rips. My imagination was getting away from me. That was all.

I moved through the room, looking for Malse. Questions burned on the tip of my tongue, and even though the head seamstress hadn't seemed open to questions, I didn't know who else to ask. I followed the sound of her voice and flinched when I stumbled on her yelling at a young man. He kept his eyes down, only nodding in response to Malse's words. His pointed ears were filled with jewelry, and the air seemed to buzz with something I had never felt before.

I should've left and minded my own business. Fixing the shirt while shoving down my questions was safer, but my curiosity got the best of me. I studied the man, wondering what he was. Elf? Fae? Demon? Before I could figure it out, Malse stopped her scolding, snapping her attention to me.

"Out with it."

My question slithered down my throat, too afraid to face the woman in front of me. If I said nothing after accidentally eavesdropping on the conversation, it'd make things worse. I held up the shirt, deliberately blocking the seamstress from view to settle my nerves.

"This shirt might not be fixable with the pieces missing from it. Should I throw it out, or—"

Malse snatched the shredded shirt from my hands. She took her time examining it. "You're right. It's not worth fixing this, but we *never* throw out fabric. Next time, set it aside, and put it in the pile for scrap material once you are done with your work."

She shoved the shirt back into my hands, making me lose my balance. She was stronger than she looked. Malse waved her hand, indicating she was done with the conversation.

"I have another question." It was foolish to keep pressing. It was my first day working in the demon king's estate. If Malse decided I was useless, it'd give Viridian grounds to throw me onto the streets.

"Out with it. I don't have time to waste."

My heart raced, but this time the words came out with ease. "What caused these tears? I've never seen anything like it."

Malse tilted her head slowly. Her lip curled, but it looked more like a twitch than a smile. "Nothing you ever want to see with your pretty little face." She lifted her hand and dragged four fingers down her cheek. "Not if you don't want to end up with scars on your face, or so much worse."

I gulped, the fear filling my belly, but there was another strange feeling mixed in. No one had ever called me pretty before. Plenty of people reminded me I was ugly because of the extra weight on my body. I believed them, after watching the slender women get all the compliments from both men and women. Malse didn't mean to call me pretty. She meant I was unscarred. That was the only explanation that made sense.

"Since you're here anyway, take these to the master's room. He asked for fresh clothing to be delivered to him right away." Malse placed a pile of folded clothes into my hands—it was the most gentle she had been since I met her. The garments were mostly black, except for dark teal ruffles attached to the collar of the shirt. "Do you know where the master's room is?" I shook my head, and Malse clicked her tongue. "Take the first set of steps up to the third floor. Go straight and turn right when the hallway breaks off. It will be the last door on the right. Don't bother to knock. Master Viridian won't be in his room. Hurry and don't waste any more of my time." Malse pushed my lower back, shoving me towards the door.

The moment I stepped out of the sewing room, silence hit my ears. None of the clicking machines could be heard outside. I had become used to the noise in the hours I spent mending clothes, which made the silence unsettling. I hurried through the hall, looking for the stairs Malse had described. It felt like the shadows were watching me. I looked over my shoulder, expecting to see someone following me, but I was alone. After seeing the amount of bodies in the mess hall, I had expected to run into more people, but they were tucked away, probably nose deep in whatever work was assigned to them.

The first set of stairs I found was new to me. Gold railings ran along the black steps with gold embedded into them. It was elegant compared to the other stairs leading to the residents' quarters. I pressed the clothes against my chest as I took the first step. The railing looked more expensive than anything I had ever owned before, so I didn't want to risk smudging the metal with my human fingers.

By the time I made it to the third floor, there was a pain in my side. I forced my breathing to slow, despite the protest in my body. There was no one to hear my heavy breathing—to hear how out of shape I was—but it had become habit to pretend I was normal. I looked around for any signs of life, but this area was quieter than the other areas of the estate.

I stepped lightly, making as little sound as possible, but my worn shoes were desperate to squeak against the smooth floors. The white walls were barren, making them look the same as every other area. I looked for any decorations that marked where I was, but there were none. It wasn't long before I reached the end of the hall. A second hallway ran perpendicular to the one I was in. It looked the same in either direction, but I turned right, as Malse instructed.

THE DEMON KING'S PET

The door at the end was larger than the other doors. It was made of black wood. Gold inlets swirled among the black in seemingly random patterns. I took a steadying breath and grabbed the gold door handle. The door swung open soundlessly, and my eyes instantly fell onto a figure in the middle of the room.

He was large. Bigger than large. And he was naked, leaving his backside completely exposed. His caramel skin stretched over thick muscles on his broad shoulders. Four black wings sprouted from his spine between his shoulder blades, stretching far on either side of him. Large horns swirled out of his head on either side of his maroon hair. A black tail extended from above his perfectly shaped bottom and went nearly to the floor, coming to a point at the end.

The muscles in his body tensed, making my body freeze. His power radiated out from him, filling every inch of the air, even the air in my lungs. It was a strong and electrifying magic, and I knew I was powerless in the face of the demon in front of me.

He turned around slowly, revealing his entire body to me. The moment his golden eyes hit mine, I realized I had seen him before. I wasn't standing in Viridian's room. I was standing in front of the demon king.

Chapter 4

The demon king looked me up and down, not phased by the fact that he was completely naked in the presence of a stranger. My eyes broke free from his, moving lower until they fell upon the startling large manhood dangling between his legs. It twitched, and my heart jolted. I looked back at the demon king's face, unable to stop the heat from crawling up my neck, making it more difficult to breathe.

"I don't think we've met before." He smiled, and it was softer than I would've expected from a demon.

I imagined sharp teeth devouring me in a couple of bites. Rumors about the demon king were dark. He ate babies for dessert. Any woman he took to his bed never woke up again. He killed whoever whenever the mood struck him. Yet, looking at him, I saw none of that on his soft lips.

I waited for my senses to kick in, to tell me to run as they had when I faced Viridian. Instead, my heart raced—from fear or something else. I wasn't sure. All I knew was I was breaking rule three, and the thought of Viridian finding out terrified me.

The blood drained from my face as a harsh realization washed over me. Viridian worked for the demon king. Either the king would tell the master of the house, or he'd punish me himself. The king was the one who had made the rules for Ethlow, so there was no escaping.

The demon king took a step forward and reached out his hand. "You don't have to be afraid of me. I won't hurt you."

I didn't trust him. He was the demon king, one of five descendants of the ruler of the netherworld. He could kill me without touching me. I was in danger, yet part of me wanted to step forward and take his hand, wondering what it'd be like to touch a demon. I pressed the pile of clothes against my chest, forcing my hands to stay in place.

"What's your name?" the demon king asked. His voice was softer than I had expected. He didn't sound like a demon who haunted the dreams of young children. In fact, he was kind of handsome, and his smile seemed...innocent.

It was a trick. Demons weren't innocent by nature. He was messing with my head, trying to get me to let my guard down, so he could take advantage of me.

I turned and ran before I was swept up in his charms. My heart pounded harder the farther away I got from the demon king. I didn't understand how I ended up in his room. I followed Malse's instructions perfectly. Unless I remembered incorrectly. I'd have to retrace my steps to see if there was a different staircase I was supposed to take.

I turned the corner, barely slowing my pace. Something wrapped around my throat, and then my back slammed against the wall. It happened too fast for my brain to process what had occurred. My head spun from the force of hitting the wall, and my lungs were in shock, refusing to work. Glowing teal eyes focused my gaze as sharp claws dug into my neck, jolting my system.

The clothes tumbled out of my hands as alarm bells rang in my head, screaming that I was in danger, but I couldn't move. The force pinning me against the wall was unlike anything I had faced before.

"What were you doing in the demon king's private chambers?" Viridian's voice was laced with venom. He was scary before, but with his nails digging into my neck, he was terrifying.

My throat was sealed shut, either from fear or the hand wrapped around it. I opened my mouth to give the first excuse I could think of, but only a small squeak escaped.

Viridian loosened his grip a hair. "Speak." There was an unspoken threat beneath the single word. Give an answer or die.

"I got lost." It wasn't a lie.

"Try again."

My stomach twisted into several knots. The tang of blood hit my nose as liquid ran down my neck from where he held me. He was going to kill me. If I didn't give him a good enough answer. Even if I did, I wasn't sure if it'd be enough to save my life.

"I was told to bring these to your room. I must've made a wrong turn or something. I swear it was an accident. I didn't mean to break the rule." It was a miracle that I was able to sputter any words.

Viridian tightened his grip on my neck, cutting off my air supply completely. He leaned forward, brushing his lips against my ear.

"If I ever catch you near the sire, it will be the last day you spend here."

He released me, and I crashed to the floor, my legs no longer working. My entire body convulsed, fear coursing through my veins. My throat ached as air found its way into my lungs again.

Viridian hovered over me, as if he was debating if his threat was sufficient. "Never use the stairs with the golden railing. This area of the estate is forbidden. My room is located above the staircase on the other side, the one with a black railing. Take my clothes there and don't linger."

"Yes, sir." My eyes were glued to the floor. I was afraid the wrong move would make Viridian change his mind.

He said nothing else before his footsteps faded into the distance. I didn't move for several minutes, even after I was sure Viridian was gone. I couldn't get my body to relax. Everything told me to leave this place before I got myself killed. Living on the streets was better than living in a mansion with bloodthirsty demons. I knew that, yet as I got to my feet, I found myself looking down the hallway that led to the demon king's room.

The door was shut, and there were no signs of him, but there was a small and rather foolish part of me that wanted to go back to his room. The demon king had been nothing like I had imagined. Viridian's harsh and commanding nature was the perfect image of a demon. The demon king was different. He had been happy to see me, and something told me it hadn't been a trick. I regretted not taking his hand.

I also regretted stepping into his room in the first place. Blood dripped down my neck, staining my shirt. It wasn't a life-threatening injury. This time. If I wasn't careful, there wouldn't be a next time.

By the time I had finished all the work Malse gave me, my fingers ached. My hands shook as I walked back to my room to drop off the clothes Malse had handed me, saying they were mine to replace the trash I wore. She said nothing about the blood that had crusted on my neck, as if it was a normal occurrence.

My neck ached, and I felt Viridian's phantom hands wrapped around my neck. The bleeding had stopped, but the constant pulse of pain was a reminder of how fragile my life was. I had broken one of the three cardinal rules. It was an accident, but Viridian didn't care. I was lucky to be alive. I should've run straight out the front door. Staying felt like a death sentence, but so did leaving.

I dropped my new clothes off in my room, hoping they'd fit, but I was too tired and hungry to bother trying them on. I went to the mess hall, hoping to find a quick meal before returning to my room and hiding for the rest of the night. I didn't want any other accidental run-ins with the demon king. I wanted to live, even though I wasn't sure what for. Deep down, it felt like I was made for more in my life. I wasn't meant to end up as a beggar, and I wasn't meant to die at the hands of a demon. I didn't know what my pathetic life would amount to, but I'd figure that out later.

The mess hall was quiet compared to the morning. The dinner rush hadn't started, which I was grateful for. I wasn't interested in fighting others to move around. I went to the window where plates of food had been served earlier. I peered inside as beings of various shapes and sizes flitted around the room to prepare for dinner. I leaned forward in an attempt to get someone's attention, but no one looked my way.

I cleared my throat. "Excuse me?"

A curvy woman with long black hair paused what she was doing to look at me. She squinted her dark brown eyes, studying me for a moment. She set down a ladle of a thick brown liquid before stepping in front of the counter. Her hair swayed as she walked, revealing a set of gills on her neck. It was the only indication that she wasn't human.

"You're the new girl, aren't you?"

Her forwardness startled me. I hadn't expected anyone to notice me when there were at least a hundred residents at Ethlow, if not more. "How'd you know?"

"You look like a guppy in a pond of sharks." She chuckled, revealing sharpened teeth. "Plus, the cooks hear everything. People are desperate for gossip, and when a human girl shows up at the doorstep of the demon king's estate, people take note."

"Are there not many humans here?" I hadn't noticed any humans specifically, but I hadn't been looking.

"No." She laughed again. It was infectious. If my neck didn't hurt so much, I might have laughed with her. "There is a small group of humans here, but in general, they don't risk coming to Ethlow. Humans and demons are a dangerous combination, like hungry horned pelicans and dancing fruit fish. Only the truly desperate or truly ignorant come here."

Her eyes moved to my neck, and I pulled my hair forward, not wanting to bring attention to the marks on my neck that were already starting to bruise.

"My guess is that you are both," she said. "I'm Aukina, by the way. And you are...?"

"Nyri," I said.

She stepped away from the counter, and for a moment, I thought our interaction was over. Then she flitted back with a bowl in her hands. "Eat. You'll need your strength. You should also see Satella. She's the healer here, and she can take care of those nasty wounds on your neck. You don't want them to get infected."

I was grateful she didn't ask how I had gotten the wounds, because I didn't want to recount my encounter with Viridian to anyone—not after the way he threatened me. "And where can I find..." Her name already slipped my mind.

"Satella," Aukina repeated. "She's actually right over there if you want to eat with her. She looks cryptic, but she's secretly a sweetheart."

A slender woman sat at a table by herself where Aukina had pointed. She had short, dark purple hair that was a shade short of black. Her curls hung below her ears, but the under part of her hair was shaved. Black lines painted her eyes and there was a pop of green on her eyelids—the only color in her outfit. She looked angry as she ate her food.

"That's okay, I don't want to bother her." I didn't want a second scary conversation in one day.

"She looks like an evil witch, but I swear that's not the case. She's a total puppy dog beneath all of that," Aukina said. "Trust me."

I wasn't sure I could trust anyone in this place, but I wasn't about to say that out loud. I chewed on my inner cheek, fighting my nerves. Having a friend would be nice, especially a healer friend. "Thanks," I said to Aukina, but she was already gone.

With a deep breath, I wandered over to the healer. I stopped in front of her table, hesitating to sit. Satella slowly looked up at me with her sharp eyes. Her face instantly broke out into a smile.

"I don't think we've met before. Sit."

It was too late to run, so I sat down, careful not to spill my food. "I'm Nyri."

"I'm assuming you're here to talk to me about your neck?" She tapped her neck where my wounds were. I hadn't looked at them in a bit, but they must've looked bad with how people instantly noticed them.

I nodded once.

"You are the type of girl who gets herself into trouble, aren't you?" Satella interlaced her fingers and rested her head on her hands.

"I prefer to stay out of sight." I didn't like bringing extra attention to myself. I didn't know what to do when the attention was on me.

"Do you prefer to stay out of sight, or are you used to being overlooked?" Satella blinked at me with a soft smile, waiting for an answer, but I didn't have one.

I picked up a spoonful of the food in my bowl, unsure of what it was. I needed the moment to ground myself. I had never tasted anything like it before, but it was smooth and had layers of flavors that made my taste buds sing.

"Aukina makes the best soup," Satella said. "I love soup." This time when she smiled, two long fangs poked over her bottom lip.

I gulped, doubting she was the puppy dog Aukina had described.

Chapter 5

Satella's grip on my wrist was like iron as she dragged me to her room. I was convinced I was being dragged to my death, and I wasn't sure how it happened. One moment we were eating, the next, she decided she had to heal my wounds immediately. Or maybe she decided she was going to eat me instead.

We stopped in front of a small door with carvings of spiders decorating the wood. She flung the door open and dragged me inside, letting go of my hand to skitter across the floor. The door slammed shut behind us, making me jump. Satella disappeared into another small room, leaving me with nothing to do but stare at the walls and contemplate if running away was the right move or not.

Every inch of the walls was covered in wood frames with small winged creatures inside. Jumping butterflies, fanged beetles, fairy moths, dragon-horned flies—bugs. They were all bugs of different shapes, sizes, and species. It was incredible and a little creepy.

"Aren't they beautiful?" Satella stood behind me, making me jump. I hadn't heard her enter the room again.

Beautiful wasn't the word I'd use. "They're interesting. You have so many of them."

"I love bugs." Her voice went a pitch higher, and her eyes tightened with glee. "I have live ones in the other room, if you want to see."

My skin crawled at the thought. It was one thing seeing them on the wall, but the thought of seeing them move was a different story. "Maybe another time. I'm a bit worn out." It wasn't a lie. I had barely been at Ethlow for a day, but it felt like I had been there for at least a week.

"I understand. When I first got to the demon king's estate, it was overwhelming. This place is different from anywhere else I've been. It was intimidating."

"You're telling me."

Satella's face softened. "Are you having a tough time?"

The throbbing in my neck rushed to the front of my mind as I thought about Viridian's hand wrapped around my throat. "I haven't been around demons before, or any other races. My hometown is small and only has humans." My eyes went to Satella's fangs. I didn't know what she was, but I had no doubt she was stronger than me.

Satella licked her teeth. "Demons aren't as scary as humans think—well, not all of them. Although, you should never make a deal with them. They always have something up their sleeves."

"I'll keep that in mind." I looked around the room to stop myself from looking at Satella's fangs again. I wanted to ask what she was, but I wasn't sure if that'd be considered rude. "How long have you lived at Ethlow?"

"Let me think." She set the bottles she held in her hands on a work desk and waved me over. I sat on the chair in front of her, and she looked at the bottles, humming as she thought. "About five decades, I think."

"Five decades?" I sputtered. Satella looked like she was in her early twenties, if not younger.

Satella tapped the skin around her eyes. "I know. I look old for my age. It's because I get too much sun, which isn't good for me, but I love the sun and heat."

I tried to swallow my astonishment, but that was impossible. My mother was younger than her, yet Satella could be a younger sister to me. "Actually, I was thinking the opposite. I would've guessed you were younger than me."

Satella waved her hand. "That's because I'm the first vampire you've seen. If you knew what the truly beautiful vampires looked like, you would understand what I meant."

My body froze. Vampire. Vampires fed on humans.

Satella decided on a bottle and scooped a creamy salve out with her two fingers. "Don't worry. I don't feed on the unwilling. Besides, I prefer the taste of fae." She winked at me, but it didn't make me feel better. I laughed, but it sounded awkward even to me. "Come closer. I promise I won't bite."

I hesitated, unsure if I believed her. I should've turned around and left Ethlow the moment my eyes landed on Viridian, but there was no point in leaving now. I leaned forward, looking anywhere but at Satella's fangs. It was rude to stare. She swiped her fingers over the cuts on my neck, one for each of Viridian's fingers. I winced from the cold, but then the pain began to subside.

"Are you homesick?" Satella's question felt like it came from nowhere.

My heart thudded. I had tried not to think about my family, but it was hard at night when there was nothing to do. I missed Melody's laugh when I made funny faces at her. I missed the way Harlan ruffled my hair because he towered over me.

"I wasn't wanted at home." My heart cracked. I hadn't wanted to admit that. My parents were trying to do what was best for the family as a whole. I was only a burden to them.

Satella wiped her fingers on her pants. "Most of us are here because we are unwanted. It's what makes Ethlow a great place. No matter who you are, you can create a new life. It helps to find a purpose for when you're not working."

"What do you do?" I didn't know where to begin to start a new life, especially with Viridian's threat hanging over my head.

Satella gestured to my wall. "I have my bugs." There was a surprising amount of love in her eyes. The bugs were more than a simple decoration to the vampire. She cared about them.

I knew what I had to do. "Thank you for your help."

"I'm happy to help. If your neck starts hurting, come see me again."

Satella wasn't as scary as I had imagined vampires to be.

"I will," I said. I knew exactly what I wanted to do with my free time.

For how elaborate Ethlow was on the inside, I was shocked by the grounds surrounding the mansion. Simple grass covered the ground, but there was no garden. There were no flowers bringing color to the outside world. There was hardly any life, which shouldn't have been surprising. This was the *demon* king's estate. A vicious ruler who didn't care about the people of his land—that was what everyone in Narthington said.

I hadn't decided if that was true yet. If the demon king was that heartless, why would he let people who had nowhere else to go stay at his mansion? Why would he let someone like me, whose own family didn't want her, live here for free?

I thought about what Satella asked. *Are you homesick?* I didn't know how to answer that question. I loved my family, and I thought they loved me. But I never would've kicked my mother out the way she had done to me. I never would've left my father on the streets to suffer because he wasn't what I had wanted. I loved my family, but they didn't love me the same way.

A barren part of the ground made me pause on my stroll. The dirt was dark and looked rich with nutrients, despite the lack of plant life around it. I crouched down and stuck my pinky into the dirt before touching it to my tongue. It was the perfect place to grow some tomato plants and maybe a blue melon vine.

"What are you doing?" The deep voice behind me made me jump to my feet and spin around.

My blood tried to drain from my body as I stared at the demon king, making me feel dizzy. A god or goddess must have put me on their enemy list. That was the only explanation for running into the demon king twice in one day.

"I'm not breaking any rules. I was told nothing about not being allowed to grow a garden. As long as I get my work done, my free time is mine to do with as I please." I spouted my defense as I had rehearsed it a million times just in case.

The demon king tilted his head. His face was soft as he looked at me, but his eyes danced with interest. "A garden? Is that what you're planning on doing?"

My heart hammered against my chest. If Viridian somehow found out I was meeting with the demon king again, he'd kill me. I doubted he'd give me a chance to explain myself. I should've run away without another word. "I tended a garden for my family back home. I thought it'd be nice to have one here. I can give the fruit and vegetables to the cook, if it's a problem. I want something that feels like mine." There was no reason for me to tell him what I was doing or why.

"I've never been good with plants. I have a tendency to kill things." He laughed, running his fingers through his hair below his horns. He was dressed in a black suit with a dark red coat draped over his shoulders. Despite the layers of clothes covering his body, my face heated at the memory of his naked body.

A wave of fear washed over me, reminding me that I was talking to the demon king. I took a step back, my senses finally kicking in. "I have to go."

"Wait." He grabbed my arm with sharp, black nails, but his grip was soft—nothing like the master of his house. "I can hide my wings and horns if that's what's scaring you." Before I said anything, he folded his wings into his back before they disappeared completely. His horns spiraled back into his head. Without them, he could almost pass for a human, an enormous and muscular human. But there was a powerful aura about him that was anything but human.

I should've been afraid for my life. "You're the demon king. I... I can't talk to you."

His face fell, disappointment filling his eyes, but it didn't make sense. This was his estate. He was the king of Kinzlea. He made the rules of Ethlow.

"I promise I won't hurt you. You don't have to be afraid of me." As if to prove his point, he let go of me. "You can call me Zathrian, if that makes it less intimidating."

It was a trick. That was the only thing that made sense. He wanted me to let my guard down, so he could pounce. Or he was buying time for Viridian to show up and finish what he was tempted to do earlier.

Or maybe it was a test. One I was failing. "I can't. It's against the rules." I took another step back, prepared to run to my room, but my foot hit a rock. I stumbled backwards, flailing my arms to try to regain my balance, but it didn't work. I was going to hit the ground, making a fool of myself in front of the demon king.

A strong hand caught my arm, stopping me from falling and pulling me roughly in the opposite direction. My body hit a hard surface that could've been a wall, except as I looked up, I was staring into two beautiful, glowing yellow eyes.

Chapter 6

T hunder rang in my ears. If I wasn't allowed to look at the demon king, I was sure touching him was a death sentence.

"Careful now," his deep voice rumbled beneath my palm. "We wouldn't want you hurt."

I could hardly breathe as the demon king's face was merely inches away from me. He looked more human without his wings and horns, but his eyes were an unnatural yellow that he couldn't hide. His scent was unlike anything I had smelled before, like simmering coals on the verge of igniting or extinguishing.

His hand lingered on my lower back, even though I was stable. My palms pressed against his pecs, feeling the firm power beneath. Even without using magic, he was stronger than any other man I had come across. For a moment, curiosity flashed through my ignorant human brain. What would it be like to be beneath a body like his?

Then Viridian's threat replaced any curiosity.

I pulled away from the demon, and he didn't fight it. "I have to go."

"Why?" It was a simple question, one I should've ignored for my own safety.

"It's against the rules." My feet were glued to the ground, as if my body couldn't remember the threat to my life, since the wounds Viridian had left behind were healed.

"I am the demon king." He blinked at me, tilting his head slightly. It was cute, but he was a demon. Demons weren't cute.

"And I am a human. We shouldn't be in the same room." He should've understood that better than anyone. Even if he could break the rules he made, if he didn't call off his guard dog, I was the one who'd end up mauled. I took a step back, forcing my body to remember how to move.

"Wait. Please."

There was something about the way he said please that made me hesitate again. His voice was about to crack out of desperation, but it held steady and firm—like his muscular chest.

"If someone sees me with you..." I didn't know what would happen. The demon king was the one who asked me to stay. Did that mean I was still breaking the rules of Ethlow?

The demon king looked around, his eyes scanning for any unwanted eyes. "Next time, we'll meet somewhere no one will see us."

Next time... He wanted there to be a next time.

I forced myself to take another step back. "There can't be a next time. I was told—"

He grabbed my hand, making my mind go blank. His palms were rough and strong. The kind of hands I wanted all over my body. "Forget what you were told. I want to see you again."

I licked my lips. I didn't understand why, but I wanted to see him again, too. He wasn't terrifying, like Viridian. Maybe that was part of his devilish nature. Maybe he used his charms to lure foolish women to their deathbeds, like the rumors had said.

"Why?" If he wanted to make me his next meal, I doubted he'd tell me, but I couldn't understand why he'd want to see *me* again.

"Because when you first saw me, you didn't flinch." It was a simple answer, one that didn't satisfy my question.

I wanted to ask why again, but a crow cawed as it flew above us, bringing me back to the reality of the situation. I pulled my hand away. "I have to go." Two more steps back, and then I turned away from the demon king.

"At least tell me your name," he called out after me.

I thought about telling him, but if I stopped to speak to him, I wasn't sure I'd get my wits about me long enough to run away again. I didn't stop moving until I was safely in my room, but my heart raced long after I had caught my breath.

For the next three days, I looked over my shoulder everywhere I went, searching for the demon king. I didn't know if I was hoping to see him or grateful I hadn't had the misfortune of running into him again. I hadn't seen Viridian since the incident—I knew I was grateful for that. The only place I felt safe was in my room, knowing there was no risk of accidental meetings with demons.

I stepped into the mess hall, instantly scanning the room for any demons that would make me forgo my dinner. It was before the dinner rush, which had become my preferred time to enjoy my dinner. Crowds made me nervous.

"You look better, practically glowing like a lunar jellyfish." Aukina peered through the window into the kitchen.

My hand went to my neck. After Satella put the salve on the wounds, I woke up the next day with no signs of the injuries. I had never had a cut heal that fast before. "Yeah, Satella is a miracle worker."

Aukina looked at me for a moment, and it felt like she was staring into my soul. Suddenly, she looked over her shoulder and told someone she was taking a break. She grabbed two plates and slipped out of the kitchen. She motioned for me to follow her before leading me out of the mess hall. She used a door at the back, which led to a small courtyard that was empty.

"I like coming here to eat. It's quiet, and a nice break from the chaos of the kitchen," Aukina explained.

The grass was half dying on the ground, and there were no other plants in the area. I had expected the garden of the demon king to be immaculate, but it was the one part of the estate that was neglected.

Aukina passed me a plate, and we sat on the ground together. I didn't know what we were eating, but it was the best thing I had eaten since arriving at Ethlow. It was warm against the cold air and felt like home—not that my mother ever cooked anything half as delicious. "This is incredible."

Aukina paused mid-bite, her face brightening. "It's a personal recipe of mine. I used to cook all the time for the locals back home. When I'm in the kitchen, it doesn't feel as lonely."

Loneliness was a common theme in Ethlow. "Where are you from?"

"That's a little complicated." She bit into the bread, chewing slowly to give her a moment. "I was born in the Hallow Sea, but I spent half my time on the Nescen Islands. My family hated how much time I spent on land. 'Mermaids were born to the sea,' my mother always said, but if mermaids were meant to only be in the sea, why do we grow legs on land?"

My eyes went to the gills on her neck. "How did you end up here?" I wasn't sure if that question was appropriate to ask the residents, but my curiosity got the best of me.

Aukina's smile faltered. "The humans on the Nescen Islands never accepted me because I was born in the sea, and my people didn't accept me because I spent too much time on land. One day, it all became too much, so I left. I heard about Ethlow, and I haven't thought about going home once."

My body tensed. The Nescen Islands were one of the few places bleeding heart lilies were known to grow, but I couldn't ask the mermaid about a flower when she was talking about her past. "You don't miss it?" My chest ached at night, thinking about my family back home. I wasn't sure which was worse: missing them or knowing they didn't want me.

"Sometimes," she admitted. "Especially in the summer when the flowers are in full bloom, but I never felt like I fit in there.

Here, no one fits in, which makes me feel like I belong. It probably sounds a little crazy, huh?"

I didn't know if I understood. I had never felt like I belonged anywhere because of my size. I didn't feel like I belonged at Ethlow because I was human. "No, not crazy, but don't you ever get scared living here?"

Aukina laughed. "Why would I be scared?"

Maybe it was different for a mermaid who had been exposed to other races. I looked around to make sure we were alone. "Because of the demons."

Aukina laughed again. "The demons in Kinzlea are nothing to fear. Maybe in the other kingdoms it's different, but there is an understanding in Ethlow that you don't target other residents."

"But what about Viridian? He said if I broke the rules, I would be punished." Even though the marks on my neck were gone, the thought of Viridian brought a phantom feeling of his hand around my neck.

"Sure, but it's not that hard to follow the rules. Do your work. Don't go outside. Don't bother the demon king. There are other unspoken rules, too, but those are common courtesy. You don't seem like the type that would have issues with that."

"But what if you run into the demon king by accident?"

Aukina stopped eating. "That doesn't happen. He stays in his part of the estate and doesn't mingle with us. I have never seen him in the five years I've been here."

I opened my mouth to tell her that couldn't be right. In the first two days at Ethlow, I saw the demon king three times. Surely,

I wasn't the only one running into the king. I closed my mouth again before saying anything. Maybe it wasn't a coincidence or bad luck that I had seen the demon king that many times. Heat crawled up my neck as I thought about the demon king seeking me out.

"Is that why you look like you haven't been sleeping well?" Aukina asked when I didn't say anything.

I touched the skin under my eyes. I hadn't been sleeping well, but it wasn't one thing that made me toss and turn at night. "I can't get kicked out of here. I don't have anywhere else to go."

Aukina reached over and placed her hand on mine. "Don't worry. Few get kicked out of Ethlow. In fact, I don't think anyone has been kicked out since I arrived. I know it might be a lot, but you shouldn't worry so much. You have a friend now, and you might look different, but we're all just fish trying to survive in this pond."

I looked at Aukina's tan skin compared to mine. Her hand was cold, but the gesture was warm. She looked different than me in every way except one. She also had extra weight on her body, but she looked beautiful. In that sense, even her weight looked different.

"I'm not sure a simple human fits in here." Not among the vampires who were half a decade old and mermaids who liked to live on land. Or the demons who could crush me with a snap of their fingers.

"Don't undersell yourself. You are not a simple human."

I furrowed my brows, unsure of what she meant by that. "But I am."

Aukina paused. She narrowed her eyes as if she was searching for something I couldn't see. She took her hand back, but her face was twisted with confusion. "With your magic, that makes you stand out against the others here."

My confusion only deepened. "I don't have magic."

Aukina opened her mouth, but she changed her mind. She pursed her lips before shaking her head. "Oh, well, either way, don't be afraid. It won't be long before you find your way here, little guppy, and maybe you'll even consider this place your home."

I smiled, but it felt hollow. Narthington was my home, and it was difficult to imagine living anywhere else. I hoped Aukina was right. If I kept my head down and didn't bring Viridian's attention to myself, maybe I could live a quiet, happy life here. Only, I wasn't sure if that was something I'd be able to do.

I fiddled with the seeds in my pocket, returning to the spot where I had decided to start a garden. I hadn't returned for fear of running into the demon king again. I told myself I had to avoid him at all costs, but there was a curiosity crawling up my spine. In five years, Aukina hadn't seen the demon king once. I refused to believe seeing him three times in a few days wasn't a coincidence.

The courtyard was empty as I strolled through the grass. It was a little chilly, since spring wasn't in full bloom. Ethlow was south of Narthington, so it was colder here than back home. My clothes weren't much protection against the breeze threatening the weather to become winter-like for the night, but I gritted my teeth and kept moving.

I knelt on the ground near the patch of dirt that was perfect to start a garden. All of my gardening tools were back home. They hadn't been essential to bring, but I wished I had at least grabbed a shovel. The ground was soft enough that I used my fingers to create small holes for the seeds. I listened to my surroundings the entire time, waiting for footsteps to approach—hoping for footsteps to approach—but only silence filled the air.

It was foolish to think the demon king was seeking me out. I was nothing special. I was a mere human whose family didn't even want her. It was coincidence or bad luck that I ran into the one being I wasn't supposed to see.

Dirt caked under my nails as I finished planting the last seed I had brought. Gardening gave me a purpose. The kitchen seemed to have an endless supply of food, but I could grow fresh produce for Aukina. She was my friend, and I would make other friends here. A quiet, simple life was all I needed.

At least that was what I had told myself.

There was a part of me that wanted to feel special for once in my life. The thought of the demon king seeking me out was thrilling and terrifying all at once.

I brushed the dirt off my hands as I tried to swallow the jagged truth. I wasn't someone who could pull the attention of the demon king. I pressed my palms into my knees and stood. A shadow moved across the ground, swallowing my body in the sudden darkness. The air thickened with a strange power, and my body froze as my instincts kicked in.

Danger.

I took a slow breath, preparing to run. I couldn't risk looking behind me. I took off, but I didn't make it three steps before a strong grip took my wrist, spinning me backwards. I hit a firm body, and once again I stared into the brilliant eyes of the demon king.

Chapter 7

I wasn't crazy. That was the only thought that filled my head as the demon king looked down at me. His horns and wings were nowhere in sight, but he didn't need them to make my heart race. He held my wrist tightly enough to remind me that I had no power against him, but I didn't break his gaze. I didn't want to show him I was afraid, even as my heart thundered in my ears.

"Come with me." He dragged me away, giving me no choice.

We moved away from the mansion towards a cluster of trees filling the grounds. We weaved through the trees, the demon king offering no explanation as to where we were going. I didn't bother asking, unsure if it mattered. He was the demon king, and even though being this close to him was against the rules, I was at his mercy.

Between the trees, glimpses of a glass building flashed into view. I had never seen a building completely made of glass, but I had read about them. I couldn't pull my eyes away from it as we approached. We didn't stop until we slipped inside a door that was barely on its hinges. The demon king slowed his pace, but he didn't let go of my hand, even when we stopped moving altogether.

I looked anywhere but at the demon who held my hand. There were vines that had once crawled up the side of the glass, but they had shriveled and died since. All plants inside looked the same, as if there was once someone who had cared for their lives, but they had since moved on. The only living thing that remained were rows of trees, but they were barely clinging to life.

"What is this place?" My voice was loud in the quiet building. It felt like speaking in a graveyard.

"It's the greenhouse." When I wasn't looking at him, it was easy to imagine he wasn't a demon, but that didn't make my heart slow down. He was a male, a population I had little practice with outside my brother.

"A greenhouse," I repeated. I had read about them at the old library, but only the rich had the funds to create something like that, and no one in Narthington was rich. "It looks abandoned."

"It is."

I slowly looked back at the king demon, and my breath hitched. The lighting made him look stunning. The sun reflected off his red hair like the end of a sunset. His eyes looked like the sun.

"Why did you bring me here?" My heart knocked on my ribs, making it hard to breathe.

He brushed his thumb over the back of my hand, sending a shiver up my spine. "You were worried about breaking the rules. Here, no one will see you breaking any rules."

My throat went dry. The rules. I couldn't afford to get kicked out of Ethlow. I took a step back, pulling my hand free from the demon king. "I can't be here."

His face fell as his hand fell to his side. "I won't hurt you, if that's what you're worried about."

"It's not you I'm worried about. It's—" I cut myself off, but I wasn't sure why. It felt as if I spoke Viridian's name, he'd appear at the sound of it. "You're the demon king, and I'm just... I'm just me. Why do you want to spend time with me?"

He tilted his head slowly. His eyes bore into mine, making me feel exposed, but I couldn't bring myself to look away. "Why shouldn't I?"

I had a list of reasons why, but saying them out loud felt embarrassing. "You're the demon king, and—"

"Call me Zathrian."

My mouth gaped open. This was the second time he had said that to me, but it felt wrong to call him by his name. "You're King Zathrian, and—"

"No, Nyri." I hadn't told him my name, but he had learned it anyway. I shouldn't have been surprised. He was the demon king. He moved closer and grabbed my chin, brushing his thumb over my lower lip. "Just Zathrian. Right now, I don't want you to think of me as a king."

I wanted to brush my tongue over my lip where his thumb lingered. I wanted to know what he tasted like. Instead, I stepped back. "I don't know what games you're playing, but I'm not interested. I can't afford to get caught with you, because if I'm forced to leave Ethlow, I have nowhere else to go." My voice cracked, and I silently scolded myself for being so emotional.

"I'm not playing games."

"All demons play games." I regretted the words the moment they slipped out of my mouth. The pain that twisted the demon king's face made guilt shock my heart.

"I thought this form would make you less afraid of me, but you can't see past me being a demon, can you?" His jaw tightened.

I paused, his words throwing me off. "I don't care that you're a demon." My words surprised me. I thought demons were terrifying, but even as I was alone with the demon king, the demon that was the most powerful in Kinzlea, I wasn't afraid.

He took a step forward, and his wings sprouted from his back as his horns grew out of his skull. His eyes darkened a shade, and even his skin turned a shade deeper. Sharp fangs replaced his regular canines. He spread his arms, hovering over me. "So this doesn't scare you?"

It was a test, one I wasn't prepared for. I looked at the demon in front of me, waiting for the fear to come. Being in the same room as Viridian made it hard to breathe and threatened my sanity. Standing in front of the demon king—Zathrian—made it hard to breathe, but it wasn't out of fear.

I stepped forward, closing the distance between us. There was a small voice in the back of my head that told me to run. Anything else was stupid. Yet... I reached my hand out. I ran my fingers over his horns, barely able to reach them from his towering height. His horns were smooth, except the indents where gold was inlaid.

"I'm not afraid of you," I whispered. It made no sense, but it was true.

Zathrian grabbed my chin and pulled me closer. It wouldn't take much for him to bury his teeth into my neck. "Maybe you should be afraid of me." His breath was warm against my skin, making it impossible to feel the fear I should've felt.

"Why? What will you do to me?" I licked my lips as I stared up at him.

A low growl escaped his throat. It was more animalistic than anything else he had done, but it didn't scare me. "Don't ask me questions like that."

"Why?" It was a simple question, but the burning behind Zathrian's eyes told me otherwise.

He whipped his tail around and wrapped it around my thigh, forcing me to take another step forward. The distance between us was practically nonexistent. As he spoke, his tail moved higher, sliding up my thighs and causing sensations to run through my body that I had never felt before.

"Because it makes it very *hard* to stop myself from touching you more." He licked his lips, and I had to bite my own to stop me from leaning in.

I needed space to clear my head. I knew I wasn't thinking straight, but I couldn't will myself to break free from his spell. The touch of a male was something I had craved for so long that I had tried to convince myself it wasn't in the cards for someone like me. Most men saw right through me because of the extra layers of fat on my body. Even the one experience I had had was quickly ruined once he saw what was beneath my clothes. The demon king didn't look through me, though. He looked right at me, making me feel seen in the way I had wanted one person to look at me like.

I was playing a dangerous game. It wasn't some man looking at me. It was the demon king. Demons and humans didn't mix well. There was a part of me that knew that, but every other part ignored that voice.

"Maybe you shouldn't stop yourself," I whispered. I was insane. It was the only explanation for the words that escaped my mouth before my head could stop them.

Zathrian slid his hand around the back of my neck, and before I had a second to process, his lips were pressed against mine. His mouth was hot and needy. His tongue swiped against my mouth, but it didn't feel human. I parted my mouth, and his forked tongue brushed against mine. It was unlike any other kiss I had shared before, but I found myself leaning in to his touch, needing more.

His free hand slid down my side, feeling every curve in my body. My breath hitched as I prepared for him to comment on the shape of my body. It wouldn't have been the first time a man made such a comment, but Zathrian didn't stop. His hand moved lower, cupping my bottom and squeezing hard enough that a muffled moan escaped my lips.

Shame filled my cheeks, making them burn. I had lost my mind. I tried to pull away, but Zathrian's tail pulled me closer. It moved up my legs, sliding between my thighs. I leaned into his touch, unable to think about stopping again. My fingers ran over his muscular chest, and I wondered what was beneath his clothes. Before my thoughts could go any further, he pulled away.

Zathrian was as breathless as me. He unwrapped his tail, but his fingers rested on my hips, as if he was hesitant to let go. It didn't feel real. No one had looked at me with the kind of longing in the demon king's eyes.

My senses slowly came back to me. I stepped away from Zathrian, before my impulses pulled him closer. "I should go." My voice was soft and resistant. I didn't want to leave, but I needed a moment to wrap my head around what had happened.

Zathrian didn't respond. His shoulders sank, and his jaw tensed. Disappointment flashed through his eyes.

I took another step back before I changed my mind about leaving. I couldn't let myself get tangled with the demon king—the one person I was told to stay away from. Several more steps took me away from the demon king. As I turned my back on him, I waited for him to ask me to stay, knowing I would've done as he asked, especially as my core longed for more of his touch.

I reached the door without him uttering a word. It was best to slip away without saying anything, but I found myself turning back for one last look. As his golden eyes met mine, I hesitated.

"Meet me here again tomorrow after dinner?" I turned and ran before he responded. I wasn't sure if I could handle his answer, no matter what it was.

I didn't stop running, even as I made it back to the mansion. I threw the back door open, freezing as Viridian stood in my pathway. His eyes burned into mine, anger filling his teal irises. I was dead.

Chapter 8

He knew. I didn't know how, but Viridian *knew* I broke the third and most important rule of Ethlow.

"You're cutting it close," he said. His body was unnaturally still. The hair on the back of my neck rose as if I was facing a predator.

I tried to slow my racing heart, but I couldn't take deep breaths to calm myself. I didn't want Viridian to know I had something to hide. "What do you mean?" My voice gave me away instantly.

"It's sunset."

The golden hues of the setting sun pierced through the windows, emphasizing his point. I had been too wrapped up in touching the demon king—Zathrian—to notice how late it had gotten. "That's why I was returning." I tasted the lie on my tongue. It felt obvious, but I forced my feet to hold still. If I acted like I had broken a rule, Viridian would only become more suspicious.

"I see." The demon looked at me for a moment, studying every crevice of my face. "You're playing a dangerous game. The rules are in place for a reason."

I swallowed hard, wondering if we were talking about being outside after dark. "I understand."

Viridian didn't blink as he looked at me. When he turned and walked away without another word, the weight on my chest fell to the ground. I could breathe again.

I walked to my room, resisting the urge to run. Running was suspicious. I didn't dare to look back once, even as I felt eyes following me until I shut the door to my room. I leaned against the wall and slumped to the floor. Viridian had been a simple walk away from discovering me with the demon king. I ran my fingers over my neck, reminded of the claws digging into my skin.

Meet me here again tomorrow after dinner?

Stupid.

Idiot.

Foolish human girl.

Telling the demon king to meet up with me was asking for death. Yet... My thighs ached from where his tail had pulled me closer. I brushed my fingers over my inner thigh, wishing they belonged to Zathrian.

Only once before had a man touched me with any affection, but that was different. The farm boy was kind to me until I let him see me naked. Once he had gotten what he wanted, his demeanor had changed completely.

Maybe that was all the demon king wanted.

But the way he had touched me held a desire the farm boy had never had.

I moved my hand higher, tracing the path the demon king had taken. His touch had been gentle and firm, as if he wanted me and treasured me at the same time. That feeling had been imagined.

The demon king knew nothing about me. There was no reason for him to treasure me. I knew that, yet...

My hand moved higher, and my breath became ragged. His touch had lit a fire. I wanted to know what it felt like, even though it was against the rules. Every other time I had run into the demon king, it was accidental on my end, but if I showed up at the greenhouse tomorrow, and he was waiting for me, I couldn't claim that same ignorance.

I bit my lip as my hand brushed between my legs. Zathrian hadn't touched me there, but he had been so close. I tasted blood as I thought about what it would've felt like for his tail to move a little higher than it did. I wanted his touch so much that logic flew out the window. I knew I was going to meet the demon king again, even if it was the biggest mistake I ever made.

Rain trickled outside as thick clouds covered the sky as far as I could see, which wasn't far. A thick mist hung close to the ground, making it impossible to see the trees at the back of the house.

"I love weather like this," Aukina said, setting a bowl in front of me. It was before the dinner rush, so she had a few minutes free. We sat inside the mess hall to avoid the rain.

"I hate this weather." Satella wrinkled her nose as she approached the table. She slid onto the bench next to the cook.

"I thought vampires preferred weather that blocked the sun," Aukina said. She pushed her bowl towards Satella, but the healer waved it away.

"You're stereotyping us. The sun weakens us, but it doesn't mean we hate it."

"You're the only vampire I've met that likes the sun."

Satella clicked her tongue before turning to me. "You look gloomy. Do you also hate the rain?"

I forced myself to look at the vampire. "I like rain." I couldn't stop thinking about whether or not the rain would stop Zathrian from meeting me in the greenhouse, but I wasn't about to tell them that. I didn't know Satella and Aukina well enough to trust them with a secret of that magnitude.

"Are you homesick?" Aukina asked. She shoved a piece of bread into my hand. I hadn't bothered to get food yet.

I nibbled on the bread. Last night was the first night since arriving at Ethlow that I hadn't thought about my family. "Something like that."

Aukina and Satella shared a look. I hadn't said much about my family since arriving at Ethlow. Despite everything that happened, I loved them. I didn't want to disparage their memory. However, the way the two of them looked at me, it was clear they knew there was more I wasn't telling them.

"What happens to someone who breaks one of the three rules?" I asked.

"It doesn't happen here," Aukina said. "People choose to leave of their own free will before they break one of the rules."

"There was one person who broke the rules decades ago," Satella said.

Aukina shot the vampire a look, one that warned her to shut up, but it only made me curious.

"What happened?" I prompted.

Satella ignored Aukina's silent warnings. "Don't know, but there were some residents who claimed they heard her screams in the middle of the night. The next morning, the only thing left of her was a puddle of her blood."

I leaned forward, eager to hear more. "Which rule did she break?"

"It doesn't matter," Aukina interrupted. "As long as you don't break the rules, then there's nothing to worry about. And there's no reason to break the rules. They are in place for a reason. The first rule is to protect Ethlow. The second is to protect yourself."

I waited for her explanation of the third rule, but she stopped talking. "What about the rule about the demon king?" It was dangerous to ask about that where others could overhear. If anyone learned about my interest in the demon king, they could report me to Viridian. But maybe that didn't matter. Zathrian was the king of Ethlow. If he wanted to spend time with me, maybe he'd make an exception to the rule for me.

"I don't know," Aukina admitted. "It's not like it matters. He never leaves his area of the estate."

"I saw him once," Satella said.

Aukina's eyes widened, and she quickly looked around. "Don't say something like that."

"It's not like it happened on purpose," Satella said. "It was in the middle of the night, when most people are sleeping. I was wandering the halls because I felt especially restless, but then I heard someone approaching. I slipped into the shadows out of curiosity, and then the king passed by. He looked absolutely terrifying."

"We shouldn't be talking about this. What if someone overhears you?" Aukina chewed on her nail, scanning the room for any listening ears.

Satella waved her hand. "It's not like I went looking for him on purpose. Besides, I averted my eyes the moment I saw him. For all I know, it wasn't even him."

Aukina let out a heavy breath through her nose. "Maybe you shouldn't go around saying it was him then. You don't want to end up like—" Aukina shut her mouth, realizing she was about to say something she shouldn't.

"Like?" I leaned in, needing to know what she was about to say.

Aukina cleared her throat and straightened her spine. "I need to get back to the kitchen."

I looked at Satella, but her eyes were averted.

"I should head back to my room. The rain is making me feel faint." The vampire stood, and she and Aukina left at the same time.

I looked back at the window, watching the rain hit the glass. It felt as if the weather was a bad omen, telling me to avoid the demon king.

My hair was drenched by the time I made it to the greenhouse. The rain pounded against the glass ceiling, showing where all the leaks were. The pitter-patter of raindrops drowned out the sound of birds and everything else that was usually in the background. I could barely hear my own footsteps as I avoided the pieces of broken glass that covered the path. Rows of tables filled the center of the building, making it impossible to wander freely.

I scanned the open areas for signs of the demon king, but there were none. In the back, rows of trees blocked the view of the rest of the building. The cracks in the ceiling hung above the trees, allowing the water to drip down and give the trees life. It was the reason they had survived when everything else died. I was drawn to the only life in the building.

I touched the leaves, feeling the life in the tree. They were alive, but they weren't happy. They needed fertilizer and a good pruning. A few simple touches could make them thrive instead of surviving. I could give life to the greenhouse. I closed my eyes, imagining healthy, green leaves and beautiful pops of flowers filling the building. I could practically taste the life that waited for me.

A crack of thunder made my eyes snap open. My eyes immediately landed on a pair of golden eyes, staring at me from the next row of trees. I took a step to the side to get a better view of Zathrian, but the trees were too overgrown, making it nearly impossible to see him.

"You came," I said. I walked slowly, looking for a proper opening in the row of trees.

"You asked me to." His footsteps followed mine.

My heart pulsed like the waves of raindrops falling on the ceiling. "I wasn't sure if you'd come because of the weather."

I couldn't tear my eyes away from the trees separating us, eager for a glimpse of the demon king.

"I wasn't sure if you'd show up at all."

I lost sight of him, making me stop. I leaned to the side, trying to look through the trees for his burning red hair, but even his footsteps had disappeared.

"I didn't know if I was going to come, either," I said.

"Then why did you?" His voice came from right behind me.

I spun around and had to look up to see his face. There were only a few inches between us. He was wearing a different outfit than before. Gold strips of metal covered most of his neck in a broad collar. Chains of a matching color hooked to the bottom of it and ran down his bare torso. My eyes were no longer focused on his face as his caramel skin glimmered from lingering rain over his torso. There was little room for imagination, even below his hips. His muscles formed the shape of a v below a skirt-like piece of fabric that was completely void of color.

I swallowed, but my throat was dry.

"I don't know," I whispered, unable to pull my eyes back to his face. "Your outfit is... interesting."

A deep rumble echoed from his chest as he chuckled. "Do you like it?"

ERI EVERLAND

I didn't want to admit the truth. No one wore outfits that scandalous in Narthington. I wasn't sure anything would get done if they did—not that any of them had a body like the demon king. I cleared my throat and forced my attention back to his face. Instead of answering him, I asked, "Why aren't the residents of Ethlow allowed to interact with you?"

His brows rose, surprise dancing across his eyes. "For safety reasons."

I moved away from, afraid my hands would move on their own if I didn't put some distance between the demon king and myself. "Mine or yours?"

Silence answered me. His footsteps crunched behind mine as he followed me closely. Even though I couldn't see him, I was painfully aware of each of his movements, every step, every breath.

"What happens if someone learns I'm breaking the rules?" I asked. "Will I get punished?"

"It's... possible."

I stopped, spinning around. Zathrian nearly ran into me, not expecting me to stop suddenly.

"Are you going to punish me for breaking the rules? You are the one who created them, right?" The scent of ash and burning embers filled my nose as I moved closer to the demon king.

"Do you want me to punish you?" His lips tugged into a smirk, making my heart stutter.

"Yes."

Chapter 9

I slapped my hands over my mouth, unsure of why I said yes to that. "I didn't mean that."

"That's a shame." Zathrian lifted my chin up with his thumb, gently pulling me closer to him. "You might actually enjoy my punishment."

My legs wobbled beneath me. I couldn't find any words. I couldn't move, entranced by the golden eyes piercing my soul.

Zathrian leaned forward. His breath caressed my ear as he spoke. "I didn't think you'd like that, my pet." He nipped my ear, and a soft moan escaped my mouth.

I was clay in his hands, ready for him to mold me in whatever way he wanted. I lifted my hands to his chest, surprised by how smooth his skin was. I had expected a demon's skin to feel rougher, but I wanted to run my hands all over his body. I didn't know what was wrong with me. I had always done the right thing. I smiled politely at the neighbors, made friendly conversation with the gentlemen at the market, and did everything my mother had asked. I was a good girl.

None of that mattered. The neighbors judged me for my looks. The gentlemen never saw past my looks. My family tossed me aside like I meant nothing to them. For once, I wanted to break the rules and live my life.

Zathrian groaned in my ear as my fingers traced his rippling muscles. "Careful, Nyri. If you don't stop—"

"You'll what?" I asked, earning another groan. I didn't know my way around a male body, at least not well. The one time I had been intimate with a man, it had ended as quickly as it started, and he had blamed me for the briefness, saying he would've lasted longer if I had been more attractive.

Zathrian spun me around so my back was to him and wrapped his hand around my throat. His grip was tight enough to tell me that he was in charge, but he didn't restrict my airway. "You're playing a dangerous game." I should've been afraid, especially after what Viridian had threatened, but Zathrian didn't scare me. He excited me.

His other hand snaked around my torso, pressing against my stomach. Panic rose in my throat. I didn't want Zathrian to feel the rolls on my body, but it was too late. He pulled me flushed against him, and I felt something hard press against my backside.

"Can you feel what you're doing to me?" he whispered in my ear.

I felt it, but I struggled to believe it. I wasn't the girl that drove men crazy. I was the girl in the background that hardly anyone noticed.

"Answer me, Nyri." My name on his tongue sent a surge of desire down my spine. His hand moved lower, distracting my thoughts.

"Yes," I barely managed to sputter.

He took a strangled breath in my ear, revealing just how much he was struggling. "I should walk away from you right now for both of our sakes."

The thought of him walking away made my chest ache. Nothing good could come from dallying with the demon king, but there was nothing good left in my life. I was tired of living the quiet life of a good girl. I was tired of waiting in the shadows while others enjoyed their lives.

I shifted, pressing my butt backwards, earning a groan in the process. "No one has to know. This could be our little secret."

He drummed his fingers against my throat. "This is a dangerous game, one I don't think you are prepared for."

I spun around and looked up at him. I placed my palms on his pecs and then lowered them until I was tracing the V-shaped muscles. My fingers lingered over the hem of his pants. "Then walk away." I didn't know what had gotten into me. I never imagined myself the type of woman who would openly invite danger into her life, but there I was, taunting the demon king with the simple touch of my fingers.

Zathrian grabbed my hands, stopping me from moving any lower. "Do you realize who you are touching? Most would lose their fingers for touching demon royalty like that."

A pulse of fear rushed through me, my senses coming back briefly. Zathrian was royalty, one of five descendants of the ruler of the netherworld. I knew Zathrian was the king, but what that meant hadn't fully sunk in.

"I'm sorry. I don't know what got into me. Of course, you wouldn't want a commoner touching you like that." I tried to pull my hand away, but Zathrian tightened his grip.

He guided my hand lower, pressing it against his manhood. He was hard beneath my touch, only a thin piece of fabric separating my hand from direct contact. "Does it feel like I don't want you?"

"I just— I, uh." I struggled to find words. My mouth watered as I felt him twitch beneath my touch. He was bigger than the farm boy. Much bigger. It was thrilling and terrifying, and I didn't know what to do.

"If you don't believe me, let me show you how much I want you." His hand snaked into my hair, and he tugged me closer to him until his lips met mine. He pushed his tongue into my mouth, and I parted my lips, giving him anything he wanted.

Zathrian's other hand moved to my chest, his hand covering my plentiful breast. He squeezed, sending a rush of pleasure through my nerves. I moaned into his mouth, and he lapped up the response. He continued kneading my breast and ravishing my mouth, completely swarming my senses from his touch. When something tugged at my pants, I yelped, but Zathrian refused to let me pull away.

"Relax," he whispered before capturing my mouth again.

It was his tail. The realization hit me like a boulder. I barely paid attention to Zathrian's hands as his tail slid inside my pants and undergarments in one fell swoop. It continued moving down until it was between my legs. Even with my thighs pressed together, his tail continued moving, unbothered by the extra girth around my legs. His tail moved deeper until it hit—

A loud moan filled the air as his tail found my heat, slick with arousal. It moved slowly, exploring my folds, searching for the spot that made my legs quiver. I barely noticed when Zathrian stopped kissing me to watch my face twist with pleasure. His tail flicked back and forth over my bundle of nerves. No one had ever touched me there, and my head swirled with pleasure.

"Breathe," Zathrian whispered into my ear. I hadn't realized I had stopped breathing, but at the demon king's command, I gasped for air. My chest heaved up and down as pleasure overtook all of my senses. It was unlike anything I had experienced before. "That's it, my pet."

That was the second time he called me that, but I could hardly think.

His tail moved lower and lower until he found my entrance. A small cry escaped my mouth as he pushed in a little, testing it out. I cracked my eyes open and found myself completely mesmerized by his glowing eyes. I never thought I'd find a demon handsome, let alone breathtaking.

He hesitated, his eyes searching my face for any signs of pain. "Don't stop." It was a small plea, but that was all he needed to pull out before plunging his tail deeper.

I dug my fingers into his shoulders as a new kind of pleasure pulsed between my thighs. My legs turned to jello, and I could barely stand as Zathrian pumped his tail in and out of me. Zathrian held onto me, keeping me up right, but he didn't slow down for a second. His tail continued moving in and out of my entrance, and at the same time, it rubbed over my bundle of nerves. The combination was too much for my body to handle.

The wave that crashed over me was unlike anything I had felt before. Pleasure coursed through my nerves and my muscles tightened. Once it was over, my body collapsed. Zathrian pulled his tail free and caught me, lifting me up as if I weighed nothing. No one had carried me like that in a long, long time, saying I was too heavy for anyone to pick up. The demon king didn't look the slightest bit strained as he carried me over to a bench. He set me down and then kneeled in front of me.

He pushed the hair out of my face, his touch surprisingly soft. "You make the most incredible noises."

My cheeks burned as energy bounded back into my body. I had never felt a fraction of the pleasure Zathrian had given me. With the farm boy, it had been uncomfortable the entire time to the point I had been eager for it to be over. He didn't stop to check on me once, and I had thought that was what sex was like.

Zathrian stood, leaving me on the bench. He looked over his shoulder. I leaned over to see what he was looking at, but I didn't see anything.

"I have to go." He didn't look back at me.

My chest felt like it was going to collapse. "Oh," was all I could manage to say. I didn't know what I had been expecting. He was the demon king, and I was a human. His desire to touch me didn't mean he wanted anything else to do with me.

I straightened my spine, pushing away my disappointment. I could handle that. I wasn't looking for more. Feelings were dangerous, especially when it came to a demon. I was okay with being nothing else.

"Get back inside. It's going to get dark soon." He continued, looking behind him, as if he was searching for something specific.

I ached for him to turn back and look at me one last time, but I didn't know why. "Where are you going?"

"I have business to attend to," he said. He turned and took a couple steps. I watched him the entire time, wishing he'd look back just once. He stepped into the shadows and was gone a split second later.

My pet.

At the moment, I had enjoyed being called that, but now I wasn't sure. It made me feel like nothing more than a plaything. I didn't know if I wanted to be the demon king's pet. Then again, if it meant feeling pleasure like I had, maybe it wasn't such a bad thing.

Chapter
10

The days went by without any sightings of the demon king. He hadn't shown up at the greenhouse or anywhere else. I tried to go about the day as if it didn't matter. It was better if I didn't break the rules. Logically, I knew that, but I found myself looking around every corner, hoping to see a pair of golden eyes watching me. I tried to focus on sewing until I was released for the day. After dinner, I spent every moment in the greenhouse until it started to get dark. I kept my hands busy by working on cleaning up the debris. I wanted to return the greenhouse to its former glory. It had nothing to do with hoping Zathrian would show up.

On the fourth day, I woke up with a heavy weight on my chest. Zathrian said he had to go, but he never said he'd be back. I wasn't surprised that, after getting a taste of me, he had changed his mind. It wasn't the first time that had happened. It likely wouldn't be the last.

"What's wrong with you, human?" Malse looked me in the eyes. When I was sitting, she was the same height as me.

"Nothing." My voice felt empty. There was no reason to be upset. I was prepared for the thing with Zathrian to be casual. I hadn't expected him to disappear for days. He said he wanted me, but he left before he got anything from me.

"You're slow today."

"Sorry." It was hard to care about patching clothing when my mind was preoccupied.

Malse let out a long sigh. "Whatever is pulling your attention, figure it out. I don't accept sloppy work. If you're missing home, then either leave or accept your fate. Wasting your emotions on trivial things does you and everyone around you no good."

I swallowed hard. I should've been missing my family. I had never been away from them that long, but I had been too wrapped up in the demon king to think about missing my family. Guilt flushed my system. "You're right. I shouldn't waste my energy on things I can't control."

"Good. Now that you're better, I need you to deliver these to the demon king's room." Malse shoved a pile of pressed black and red clothes into my hand.

I swallowed hard. "I can't go in there." The thought of going to the demon king's room where I might see him again made my heart stutter. I wasn't sure if it was a good thing.

"You don't have a choice." The creases on Malse's face deepened. She was losing her patience.

"But why are you sending me? I haven't earned that kind of privilege yet." I wasn't ready to face Zathrian—not after he disappeared for days. I didn't want him to confirm what I feared.

The corner of Malse's lips tugged up, a rare sign of amusement from the goblin. "This isn't a reward. It's a punishment. Don't let your personal life affect your work, or you'll be made to deliver the demon king's garments daily."

My body tensed. Seeing the demon king was a punishment, because if I stumbled into him, I'd be breaking one of the three cardinal rules of Ethlow and risk my residency. Others feared running into the demon king, but I had secretly been hoping he was around every corner.

"Now you look thoroughly afraid." Malse's chuckle echoed as she walked away.

She was right. I was afraid, but not for the reason she thought. I wasn't afraid of being kicked out of Ethlow or accidentally seeing the demon king. I was afraid the demon king would take one look at me and pretend he didn't recognize me. I was afraid that I wanted to see the demon king, instead of praying to the gods and goddesses, that I wouldn't see him again. Zathrian owed me nothing. Whether or not others caught us together wouldn't affect him. But if they saw me, I could lose everything for a demon who didn't care.

Yet, I wanted to see the demon king. I wanted to see Zathrian.

My fingers curled around the clothes in my hands. I needed to rein in whatever desires swirled in my chest. Zathrian was the king. I was a homeless human girl. It was best if I left him alone, taking the days of his absence as a sign. I couldn't afford to get tangled with someone like him, anyway.

"Don't worry. She's messing with you." A man with fiery orange hair looked at me from across the room. His red eyes burned bright. No, he wasn't a man, but there were no other indicators of what he was. He had come in and out of the room, delivering baskets of torn clothes and taking mended garments away with him. I hadn't thought to ask his name. I hadn't talked to anyone who didn't approach me first, too wrapped up in my own worries to care.

"She is?" I asked, studying his figure. He was taller than most men, and his muscles were barely contained inside his simple white shirt. Dirt covered his boots, and fresh scars decorated his hands. Whatever his job at Ethlow was involved physical labor.

"Malse may not look like it, but she has a sense of humor," he said. "She's constantly pranking me and the others. One time, she even dyed our uniforms bright pink. She also cares a lot once you manage to worm your way into her heart."

It was hard to believe the man's words. "She said this was punishment." I lifted the pile of clothes to show him.

"The demon king is away on business. He's been gone for three days," he said. "Malse probably wants you to get out of this room for a bit to shake off whatever has you down."

I bit the inside of my cheek in an attempt to squelch my question, but it wasn't enough. "I'm not down. How do you know the demon king's away on business?" If he was gone, it'd explain his absence, but he didn't bother to tell me he'd be away for days. I tried to remind myself he owed me nothing. A few kisses and a heated meeting in the garden meant nothing.

"I'm part of the kingsguard at Ethlow. We get notified when he leaves, which puts us all on edge, and it's okay to not be okay."

I ignored the last part of his statement. "Why? Wouldn't you be relieved he's gone?" It was against the rules to mingle with the demon king, so I assumed his lack of presence would have been a relief. As I thought back on the past three days, Ethlow had been especially quiet.

"The demon king protects us," he said. "He keeps Ethlow safe from intruders. When he's gone, the shadows seem to move more, as if they are looking for an opportunity to strike." A shudder ran through his body as he thought about it. It made me wonder what kind of horrors he had seen during his time at Ethlow. "I'm Reamann, by the way." He offered his hand to me. I took it, and his grip was strong and steady.

"I'm Nyri."

"It's nice to meet you," he said with a brilliant smile. "If you ever need anything, ask one of the guards, and they will find me. Oh, and try not to take Malse too seriously. She really does have a good heart." He waved goodbye as he pushed a cart of clean clothes out of the room.

I waited a moment before leaving. Zathrian had been away on business for three days, which meant he wasn't avoiding me—at least there was a chance that was the case. The weight on my chest lessened as I made my way to the demon king's room. He was the one who had approached me. He was the one who was hard beneath my touch. Maybe, just maybe, a taste of me didn't revolt him.

I stopped in front of the stairs with golden railings, my hope falling into a pit of darkness. I knew exactly where Zathrian's room was, but memories of Viridian's fingers around my throat made me freeze. Even if Zathrian hadn't been avoiding me, I should've been avoiding him. I knew that, but I also knew that I didn't want to stay away.

The gold metal was cool beneath my touch. I slid my hand over the smooth railing as I ascended the stairs, desire pulling me forward. There was nothing to fear or desire. Zathrian was away on business, so going into his room meant nothing. Yet, it meant everything. My heart thundered as I made it to the top of the stairs, partially from the exertion of climbing the stairs, partially from the anticipation of entering Zathrian's room.

I held his clothes close to my chest, telling myself there was nothing to fear. I was only doing what I was told. I wasn't breaking the rules. By the time I stood in front of the large doors leading to the demon king's private quarters, I could hardly breathe. My hand shook as I reached for the door. As I opened it, a wave of air hit my face, bringing Zathrian's scent burning into my nose. It reminded me of the nights I had spent sitting in front of a dying fire.

I stepped through the door, my fears and worries burning away. I placed the clothes on his bed, but I didn't leave right away. Instead, I took in the details of his room, needing to learn more about the demon who had touched me like no other had.

The bed was set in a black frame with four posts that towered to the ceiling. Carvings of flowers decorated the bed, but they weren't regular blossoms. My fingers ran over the curves of the flowers I had seen once when I was a young child. Bleeding heart lilies—the flower that had made me want to learn more about gardening. They didn't look like regular lilies, so even in a solid black form, they were distinct. When in full bloom, bleeding heart lilies looked like a heart that had been cut, pulled open and twisted until blood poured out from the center. They couldn't grow in Narthington. It was too cold and dry there for the special flowers. They could only blossom on the southernmost islands that were warm and humid all year around, like the Nescen Islands.

Even on those islands, it took a special hand to guide the flowers to life. Most couldn't care for the rare and delicate flowers, making them cost more than gold and jewels. It was a dream of mine to see a bleeding heart lily alive and in person. The one I had seen had been dried and pressed between two pieces of glass. The merchant had been looking for a buyer, but Narthington was the wrong place for that. The flowers cost more than any of us made in a year.

Had Zathrian seen one of those flowers before? Or was his bed simply decorated with the coveted flower because of its prestige? I pulled my hand away. Zathrian was a king. He could go any-where he wanted and see the rarest of flowers. He could afford an entire garden of bleeding heart lilies if he wanted. It was another reminder of how different we were.

King and peasant.

Human and demon.

Immortal and mortal.

Handsome and me.

I took a step back, needing to leave his room. My fantasies of Zathrian wanting something more were nothing more than the foolish idealizations of an unwanted girl, desperate for the kind of love bards wrote songs about.

I turned to run out of the room and back to the sewing room, but voices echoed from the hallway. I was told to deliver clothes, so there was nothing wrong with being in the demon king's room. But when Viridian's deep voice flowed underneath the door, panic took over my senses. I looked around for a place to hide. A closet with black doors was on the other side of the room. I ran there without thinking, closing the doors as the main entrance opened.

"Can we discuss this later?" Zathrian asked.

I looked through the crack in the closet doors and watched as the demon king strode into the room. He wore the same outfit I had last seen him in, but dirt and bruises covered his torso. There were bags under his eyes, and his face was tight. He stopped in front of his bed, staring at the clothes I had dropped off.

Viridian walked through the door after the demon king, keeping his perfect posture intact. "I understand you have had a long couple of days, sire, but there are responsibilities you must attend to."

Zathrian stepped closer, barely paying attention to the master of the house. "I am the king of Kinzlea. Aren't I supposed to be the one who says what I'm supposed to do and when I do it?"

Viridian kept his composure, but the air around him darkened, as if shadows were creeping into his aura. "There are rules that even you must follow."

Zathrian picked up the pile of clothes and inhaled deeply. His eyes widened. "I know. I'm not asking to skip my responsibilities.

I am telling you that I will get to them after I've had a moment to bathe and change."

Viridian tilted his head, looking beyond the demon king to get a look at what he was holding. His nose twitched. "Is something wrong, sire?"

Zathrian turned around, and Viridian's shadows disappeared the second before the king laid eyes on him. "No. I'm ready for a moment of peace. Do I have to ask again?"

If Viridian caught onto anything strange, he didn't show it on his face. "No, sire. I will leave you be as long as you remember what we discussed."

A muscle in Zathrian's jaw feathered. Viridian was the master of the house and assistant to the demon king, but it didn't feel that way as they spoke. Viridian used the proper language to address a king, but there was an undertone of disobedience, as if Zathrian was powerless against him.

"I know," Zathrian said, but he didn't offer any other confirmation. He followed Viridian to the door, shutting and locking it behind the master. He pressed his hands against the wood and let out a long sigh. His face softened, relief replacing the annoyance that had been there a moment before.

It felt wrong to watch him in the privacy of his room, but I was stuck until he decided to leave. Malse was going to kill me for being late and slacking on my duties. If she was only teasing before, I didn't want to know what her angry side looked like.

"You shouldn't be in here." Zathrian's voice filled the room, making me freeze. He wasn't talking to me. He couldn't have been.

I didn't dare breathe. I couldn't afford to have him discover my presence.

Zathrian stood straight, frustration filling his features once again. He looked directly at the closet, his eyes meeting mine through the crack. "Are you going to continue to pretend like you're not there and insult me, or are you going to show yourself, Nyri?"

Chapter

II

Zathrian didn't move, his anger pulsing in the air. There was no point in continuing to hide. It'd only make him angrier, but I couldn't get my hands to stop shaking. I didn't know what was running through his head, but it was bad.

I pushed the door open slowly, but I didn't step out of the closet. "I didn't mean to spy on you." My mouth was dry, and no amount of swallowing helped.

Zathrian took a staggered breath. "Do you realize how dangerous that was? If he had—" He cut himself off, curling his fingers into fists.

Run. My instincts were screaming at me to leave, but I couldn't take a single step, not when Zathrian looked like that. Not when he was angry at me. I straightened my spine. I didn't want to act like a coward, even though I was terrified.

"It was an accident. I was ordered to drop your clothes off. Before I left your room, I heard the two of you outside. I panicked and hid." It was the truth, other than leaving out the part where I lingered in his sacred space because I was desperate for a scrap of him.

"You never should've been in here." Zathrian's voice was laced with ice, and it pierced my heart. Any hope that had been regained by Reamann's unknowingly kind words was shattered.

"You're right." Foolish girl.

Before my heart completely shattered, a surge of determination filled my muscles. I rushed out of the closet, aiming straight for the door. I needed to get as far away from Zathrian before he infected my thoughts, making it impossible to leave his side.

I was halfway across the room when he grabbed my arm. "Where do you think you're going?"

From that distance, a new scent filled my nose. Blood and sweat. Whatever business Zathrian attended to wasn't the normal kind of business. "I'm leaving, since I never should've been here in the first place." The sharpness in my words surprised me. I didn't talk to people like that, even when I was upset, but this was different. I was hurt, angry, and embarrassed.

Zathrian didn't let go of me, and I didn't fight him. "You don't understand. Being near me is *dangerous* for you. If you had been caught sneaking around my room, then—" He cut himself off abruptly, as if he didn't want me to know what the consequences were.

"Then what?" I pushed. "I was caught in your room by you, wasn't I? So what are my consequences?" Stupid. Foolish. I was pushing the most powerful demon in Kinzlea. I was asking for death.

"I'm not the one you need to fear." His voice was a low growl, and his eyes flickered. I was pushing him too far, yet I couldn't stop myself.

"Then who am I supposed to fear, because you're the one threatening me? You're the one who's angry and holding my arm, refusing to let me leave." My heart pounded as I stared into his eyes, unable to look away. "You're the one who left without telling me when you were coming back." There it was. The real reason I had been angry. For three days, I had felt unwanted. For three days, I could hardly think about anything other than when I'd see Zathrian again, and I hated myself for it.

"I am the *king*. I don't have to inform you of what I'm doing."

My body slumped. I knew better to get my hopes up, but that hadn't stopped me. "You're right. I'm a stupid human. Why would you tell me anything? Why would you want me? I spent the last three days hoping I'd see you around every corner, but I know I was being stupid."

Zathrian's brows furrowed, and his jaw went slack. "You were looking for me?"

There was no point in lying, not when everything was already ruined. "Yes. I thought maybe..." I paused. I didn't want to say it out loud, but it was too late to stop it. "Maybe I was special for once. Maybe you saw something in me that others didn't. Don't worry. I know it was a fantasy. I won't come back to your room. If we have the misfortune of crossing paths after this, I'll walk away. You don't have to worry about me breaking the rules any longer."

"You're right. You are a stupid woman."

My jaw fell open. I hadn't expected him to be that blunt with his words.

Zathrian pulled me closer. "If you think I'm going to let you walk away, then you are stupid."

"What—"

Zathrian's mouth was on mine before I could finish my question. Confusion filled my heart, but it quickly faded into the background as Zathrian pushed his tongue into my mouth. He grabbed the back of my thighs and picked me up. I wrapped my legs around his waist. His hardness pressing against my core, making a deep need fill every inch of my body.

Zathrian moved until my back hit the wall. He pulled his mouth away from mine, moving it to my ear. "For the past three days, all I could think about was what you would sound like with me buried deep within you." He shifted his hips, pressing them against me and making me moan. "I wanted nothing more than to come back here, rip off your clothes, and devour you in every possible way." He scraped his teeth over the sensitive spot behind my neck. "The moment I smelled you in my room, I nearly lost my mind. Do you know how difficult it was to have a normal conversation, knowing you were only a few steps away from me." He ran his tongue down my neck until he met my shirt. "You being in my room is dangerous for a number of reasons, but the worst one is that I'm not going to be able to control myself until I've touched every inch of you."

He rolled his hips against me, the friction making my eyes roll back. He ripped my shirt open, tearing it in a way that destroyed the piece of fabric, but I didn't care. Not as he moved his mouth lower, taking my nipple in his mouth. I arched my back, greedy for more. He flicked his forked tongue over the bud, grabbing my other breast with his hand. He kept me propped against the walls with his hips alone, proving his inhuman strength.

Only after his tongue tasted both of my breasts did he move. He grabbed my ass and carried me away from the wall over to his bed. He sat on the bed, keeping my legs wrapped around his waist.

"Grab my horns," he ordered.

I looked at the horns on his head, hesitating. He grabbed my wrists, guiding my hands to his head until my fingers wrapped around the base of his horns. A groan rumbled from his chest from the touch. I moved my hands up and down a little, and his cock twitched beneath me.

"Careful, pet," he muttered with his eyes half open. "Keep doing that, and I will lose any sense of control I have left."

I inhaled sharply, debating about how far to push him. I wanted to know what it was like for him to lose control, but there was a vein of fear in my chest that made me hesitate. "What if I want you to lose control?"

Everything in my life had been controlled. My purpose had been to help my family, to make sure we thrived as a whole. In that process, I had been left behind, making me crave the chaos of the world I had tried to fight. It didn't matter anymore. Being the perfect child was for nothing.

Zathrian's eyes snapped open, his lips curling into a taunting smirk. "Either you don't realize how dangerous the game you're playing is, or you're more wild than I ever imagined."

It was likely a mix of both. "I want to feel alive. I'm tired of playing by the rules." I got hurt whether I followed the rules or not. I wanted to know what it was like to not listen to my head and follow my heart.

Zathrian's eyes darkened. "Lift yourself up."

I did as ordered, using his horns to hover over his hips. He moved his hands beneath me, removing his bottoms with efficiency, as if he had done this a hundred times with a hundred other women.

I quickly pushed that thought away. Even if he had a thousand other lovers, for this moment, I was his, and that was enough. For now.

Zathrian's tail tugged at my bottoms, pulling them down. I shifted in an attempt to help, but he grabbed my waist band. "Don't." The single word made me still. With his sharp claws, he ripped through my pants and undergarments. He shredded them, leaving me completely exposed to him. Only the gold broad-collar wrapped around his neck covered any part of his skin.

His eyes looked up and down, taking in the sight of my naked body. I held my breath, resisting the urge to grab something to cover up my skin. I closed my eyes, afraid of the response from the demon king. The farm boy had taken one look at my rolls and cringed. He had fucked me anyway. I didn't want to see that same disgust in Zathrian's eyes.

Zathrian grabbed my chin with his thumb and pointer finger. "Open your eyes." I followed his orders, but my heart raced with panic. "There's no reason for you to hide."

"But I'm not beautiful." I didn't mean to say those words. Even as others called me fat and ugly, I had always ignored them, trying to act like their words didn't affect me. However, after years of being told I wasn't good enough for the world because of the fat on my body, I started to believe the harsh words.

"Whoever told you that deserves to burn in the netherworld for all eternity. From the first moment I laid eyes on you, I knew I wanted to be between your legs." His tail moved between my folds as if to emphasize his point.

It was hard to believe his words when so many others had said no one would want me, but it was also hard to deny as his tail prodded at my entrance, sending tingles running through my spine.

"And if you don't believe me, let me prove it to you," he whispered. He reached his hand between us, grabbing his cock. He moved it over my clit as his tail continued to move in and out of me. His cock was thicker than his tail, but as he moved it back and forth, playing with my sensitive bundle of nerves, all I could think about was what it would feel like to have him inside of me.

My core tightened from those thoughts. He pumped his tail in and out of me, and a familiar pressure built in my core from the sensations and thoughts mixing together. I tightened my grip on his horns, barely able to breathe, and my entire body tensed.

Zathrian groaned in my ear, pushing me over the edge. Waves of pleasure moved through my body like crashing ocean waves. I cried out as my walls pulsed around Zathrian's tail. He kept pumping in and out of me until my grip on him loosened. My chest heaved up and down. I had barely done any work, but I was exhausted.

Slowly, Zathrian pulled his tail out from between my legs. He stuck the tip in his mouth, sucking off my juices while making eye contact with me. "You taste even better than I had imagined."

A new fire burned in my core, and the exhaustion I had felt a moment before was nowhere to be found. I wanted more. I wanted to feel him slide into me and take every part of me.

"You're not done, are you?" After he had left so abruptly last time, I was afraid he'd do the same thing.

"Nothing could tear me away from you right now," he said. He moved his cock lower until it lined up with my entrance.

"But don't you have responsibilities?" I didn't know why I was fighting it. I wanted Zathrian to stay more than anything.

Zathrian cupped my face, running his thumb over my cheek. The gesture was surprisingly gentle and caring for the demon. "The only thing I care about is making you come on my cock."

I whimpered at the thought. He was so close to filling me, and I needed it. "Please."

Zathrian brushed his lips against mine and then whispered, "I want you to take control. Lower yourself onto me at your own pace." He leaned back to watch me, and my breath caught in my throat.

I had never had control like that. My heart thumped, wondering what it would feel like to go at my own pace and take charge of my pleasure. I shifted my hands on his horns to get a better grip. His breath quickened at the slight movement. The thought of giving the demon king pleasure made me bite my lower lip. I wanted to make him feel the pleasure he had made me feel.

I lowered myself onto his cock slowly, giving myself time to adjust to his size. My chest heaved, a mix of pain and pleasure. Each time I moved, Zathrian groaned. When nearly all of him was inside of me, he closed his eyes, fisting the bedsheets as if it was a struggle to resist touching me.

"Zathrian," I whispered. He snapped his eyes open, panic and pleasure mixing together.

"Are you okay?" Such a simple question, but it felt like more than that.

I nodded three times. I was nervous, but I was more than okay. I lifted myself up and then moved back down. It was slow, but faster than before. I continued that motion, moving a little faster each time. Zathrian didn't look away or close his eyes, watching every expression I made, assessing what I was feeling.

The pleasure took over my senses, making it difficult to focus on my movements. My thighs burned, and my motion became erratic. I wasn't sure how much longer I could continue, but then Zathrian grabbed my hips. His grip was strong and commanding as he lifted me up before slamming me back down. Each thrust felt better than the last, and I cried out each time he slammed me back down.

I felt the familiar buildup of pleasure, and knew I wouldn't last much longer. I stroked Zathrian's horns, wanting him to feel the same level of pleasure. Our grunts and moans mixed together, our breath tangling into one.

"Zathrian..." I said, but I couldn't find any words, my mind went blank except for the pressure that threatened to break through the dam at any second.

"Don't hold back," he said, as breathlessly as me. His mouth found mine, the final stroke needed to push me over the edge. He devoured my moans, slamming me back down on him until he let out a feral groan unlike anything I had heard before. I felt his warmth fill me, but I couldn't think or breathe as wave after wave of pleasure coursed through my veins.

Sex had never felt like *that* before. I was completely drained, and as we both quieted, my grip on the demon king's horns slipped free. Zathrian wrapped his arms around me, holding me close to him. I let myself fall into his touch and leaned my head against his chest. I listened to his heart, two distinct beating patterns filling my ears.

"You have two hearts?" I asked, unsure if I was hallucinating from exhaustion.

"Yes," Zathrian answered. He ran his fingers up and down my back, tracing my spine and lulling my body further into exhaustion.

I closed my eyes, the beat of his hearts strangely calming. I couldn't let myself fall asleep. Malse was expecting me. "I have to get back to work." I didn't try to get off Zathrian's lap. The last thing I wanted to do was return to patching clothes under the watchful eye of the goblin.

"Just rest."

I wanted to listen to him, but I pushed off his chest. "I'm already breaking one of the rules of Ethlow by being here with you. I can't ignore my responsibilities."

Zathrian's jaw tightened. He placed his hand on the back of my head, gently guiding it back to his chest. "I will take care of it. You need rest."

This time, I didn't fight him, the lure of sleep too strong.

Chapter
12

My mind wandered somewhere between sleep and consciousness. I was aware that the sheets beneath my fingers were too soft to be the ones I had been sleeping in since I arrived at Ethlow. They were too soft for my bed back in Narthington, too. It was a dream, one of luxury and love. Falling for the King of Kinzlea—the demon king—was nothing more than folly, the kind I had built walls to avoid.

My eyes snapped open, my mind crossing the boundary between dreams and reality. I stared at the black ceiling. It looked the same as the one in my room. If it weren't for the incredibly soft bed bending to every curve in my body, I could've mistaken the room for mine.

I couldn't remember how I got into the clothes clinging to my body—they were nicer than anything I owned. A soft scent of honey clung to my clean and smooth skin. I blinked, hoping the memories would come back, but all I could remember was the way Zathrian felt between my legs. My core throbbed at the memory. Anything after the burst of pleasure had slipped away to the shadow gods.

As I sat up, the ache in my body became apparent. Every muscle was sore in a way I had never experienced. The exhaustion ran deep into my bones, making me want to roll over and fall back asleep. Only I couldn't stay.

I wasn't supposed to be in the demon king's room. I wasn't supposed to speak to him, let alone fuck him, but logic had been thrown out the window the moment Zathrian had touched me. He was nowhere in sight, and my head pounded from the thoughts of the mistake I had made. I had to leave.

The windows were covered by thick curtains, making it impossible to tell what time it was. It didn't matter. I had been gone long enough that Malse would be furious I hadn't returned. I slipped out of bed, ignoring the ache in my muscles. I had to get back to my room, change into my clothes, and figure out some sort of excuse for the head seamstress. I couldn't afford to have her tell Viridian I wasn't doing my work.

I reached for the bedroom door, but it swung open before I reached it. Zathrian stood in front of me, his eyes slightly wide with shock. He held a gold tray in his hands, filled with a variety of food.

"You're awake," he said. "Where are you going?"

I licked my lips, feeling like I had been caught doing something wrong. "I have to get back to work."

"You're not going anywhere." There was no room for argument in his voice. "Sit." He motioned towards a small table in the corner of the room. It only had one chair pulled up to it. How many nights had Zathrian sat at the table by himself, eating alone because it was against the rules to mingle with the other residents?

I sat down in the large chair as ordered. I felt like a child in its massive size, but between Zathrian's height and shoulder width, he needed a large chair. Zathrian set the tray on the table before pulling up a footrest to sit on. I smiled at the sight. He looked like a giant sitting on a thimble.

"What are you laughing at?" he asked, startling me.

I dropped my smile, wondering if it was inappropriate to laugh at a demon king. I had done worse already, so I said, "You look funny sitting on something so small."

To my surprise, Zathrian's lips pulled into a small smile. "You look funny sitting in a chair twice your size."

I bit my lip, feeling nervous. We hadn't done much talking, but it was easy to speak to him. "Maybe we should switch seats."

"No. You are my guest. You deserve the best."

My cheeks heated, and I looked away, the fluttering in my chest confusing and dangerous. "I really should get back to work. Malse is probably furious that I didn't return. I'll be lucky if she lets me keep working for her."

"It's the middle of the night. The seamstress is already tucked into her bed, and if you disturb her now, she really would be furious," Zathrian said.

My eyes widened. "She's going to kill me."

"I told you I'd take care of it. Stop worrying and eat. You need your strength." He motioned to the tray of food.

I didn't feel particularly hungry, but I knew I was. I hadn't eaten dinner, and my body was exhausted from our earlier activities. I decided to start with a piece of bread, picking off small pieces. It didn't take much for my stomach to open up with a vengeance. I picked up pieces of cheese and fruit next, shoving the food into my mouth as quickly as I could. It was only after my stomach calmed down that I realized I had been eating ravenously as the demon king watched me. It was unladylike for me to eat that much that fast—my mother had drilled that into my head. I preferred to eat alone for that reason.

I slowly set down the piece of cheese I had been ready to devour. "Are you full?" Zathrian asked.

I swallowed the bits of food left in my mouth. I wasn't full, but I wasn't hungry either. It was enough that I would manage until breakfast. "I'm fine."

"You should eat more. You need to regain your energy," he said. His eyes rarely left my face. I wasn't used to someone staring at me like that.

"I shouldn't eat that much," I said.

"Why?" He tilted his head. His question had come from a place of genuine curiosity.

"I eat too much." I didn't like how much I ate, but when I tried to eat the same amount as my mother, it never felt like enough. She had always kept her slender figure with ease, but I felt cursed. I had tried to eat less food and work harder around the house, but nothing worked long enough for me to properly slim down.

Zathrian lifted the piece of cheese I had set down. "If you're hungry, then you should eat."

I took the food from his hand, but I didn't eat it right away. "If I didn't eat so much, then I wouldn't look like this." I looked down at my larger than average body, hating every part of it.

Zathrian grabbed my chin and gently guided it back to his face. "And what's wrong with the way you look?"

The answer felt blatantly obvious. Even strangers had the audacity to comment on my looks, as if they thought it was their responsibility to remind me that I was less than them because I had extra fat on my body.

I looked down, unable to look into the demon king's eyes as I admitted what tore me apart in secret. "Thin women are pretty, and I'm the opposite of that."

"Whoever told you that is shallow and can't see the true beauty of the world," Zathrian said. My eyes returned to his, and he continued on. "Do I need to remind you what you do to my body?"

I licked my lips, the offer more than appealing. If my body hadn't felt beyond exhausted, I would've taken him up on his offer instantly. Even with the exhaustion, I was tempted. I looked down at his hips. He was no longer wearing the scandalous outfit from before. Instead, he was completely covered in a deep red suit that was only a few shades away from being black. Despite the clothes covering his body, he was just as attractive. The way his clothes clung to his form was tantalizing and teasing.

A deep chuckle rumbled from Zathrian's chest. "Later, my pet. I don't want to render you completely useless for tomorrow. The head seamstress might actually throw a fit if you're out for more than a day." He released my chin, the space between us clearing my head a little.

My cheeks heated, but I shoved the cheese in my mouth to try to hide my embarrassment. "Does she know I was...with you?"

"No," he said instantly. "No one knows where you really were. I had an assistant tell her that you fell ill and was ordered to bed for the rest of the night."

I nodded, a flare of disappointment filling my chest. It made sense he'd keep the truth a secret. It was against the rules to mingle with him, so if others learned what was going on, it would only cause issues for me. But he was the demon king. He made the rules. He could make an exception for me if he wanted.

"Should I have said something else?" His face tightened as if he was worried he had upset me.

I should've shoved my feelings deep down. I knew someone like me didn't belong with a king. I wanted to believe that spending time with Zathrian was enough, even if it was in secret, but my heart longed for more. I didn't want to be the demon king's secret.

"Why did you create the rule about the residents of Ethlow avoiding you at all cost? Do you think that lowly of others?" I hadn't meant my question to sound so accusatory, but it was too late to take it back.

Zathrian froze, and I couldn't read the emotions simmering below his smooth skin. "I think the opposite of the residents of Ethlow. Everyone who comes here to start a new life is incredible. No matter what they faced in their previous lives, they kept fighting. They didn't give up when the world shoved them down repeatedly. I love seeing everyone find their place here."

His eyes faded, growing distant. A hard truth hit me. Zathrian was lonely. He loved the beings of Ethlow, but he stayed away from them. I couldn't wrap my mind around the reason why.

I resisted the urge to reach out and grab his hand. I wanted to comfort him, but I was hesitant. His answer to my next question could change everything. "If you love them, why create that rule in the first place?"

Zathrian clenched his jaw and fist. He wouldn't look at me, and it took him a long moment to speak. "I didn't create the rules of Ethlow. I am as much a prisoner to them as you are. That is why I keep you a secret."

My heart pounded in my head, like a slow, steady hammer. The way Zathrian said that made it sound like he didn't want to keep me a secret, as if he wanted to show me off to everyone. I couldn't afford to make assumptions. It was dangerous to get my hopes up. "But you're the king. I don't understand."

"I may be a demon king, but I am not the most powerful being out there. There are checks in place against powerful demons like myself."

I wanted Zathrian to look at me. I wanted to see the look on his face, so I could comfort him, but his answers only led to more questions. "How does keeping you away from the residents of your estate keep you in check?"

"Because people who have gotten involved with me in the past got hurt, which is why you're in danger being around me. The rules are in place for your protection. Not mine. And I'm taking advantage of you by seeking you out."

My heart stilled at his admission. Satella mentioned that something bad happened to the last being known to have broken the third rule of Ethlow, but Aukina had refused to let her tell me the details. I knew I needed to find out the truth. Until then, I needed to stay away from Zathrian.

Only the thought of leaving him made my heart ache.

I stood, but Zathrian continued avoiding my gaze, as if he was prepared for me to leave, like I should've. Instead, I crawled into his lap and placed my hands on his face. I forced him to look at me. "Then we need to make sure we keep this a secret, because I don't want to stay away from you."

He finally looked at me, and there was so much sorrow weighing him down. "You will get hurt." There was no *might* about his statement.

"It'll hurt to leave you," I admitted. "I would rather risk getting hurt by being by your side than know it will hurt staying away from you."

Zathrian kept his hands balled into his fists, as if it took every ounce of strength for him to stop himself from touching me. "We shouldn't do this."

I shrugged my shoulders. "Maybe not, but I've spent my life doing everything that was expected of me, and this is where it got me. I'm tired of the world telling me what I should and shouldn't do. So, if it means staying by your side, I will happily be your dirty little secret."

Zathrian's chest heaved up and down. I feared he'd tell me no and suggest we stop this altogether. Before he could respond, I lifted myself up and gently pressed my lips against his. I didn't want to force him to do anything he didn't want to, but I had to give it a shot. It didn't take much for the demon king to start kissing me back. He picked me up, carrying me to his bed.

Whatever was going on between us was too strong to deny. Whether it was desire or something more, I didn't know. All I knew was I wasn't ready to stay away from Zathrian, even if it meant my life was in danger.

Chapter
13

I could hardly keep my eyes open at breakfast, but I didn't have a choice. Even though every part of me ached, I had to work. I couldn't pretend to be sick because I was indulging in the demon king's company all night. I had to keep up my responsibilities in Ethlow if I had any hope of continuing to see Zathrian in secret.

Satella sat down across from me, making a point to set her tray on the table extra loudly. "Malse asked me to check on you yesterday, because you fell ill in the middle of the day. Something about throwing up while running errands for the seamstress. She was worried—the goblin was actually *worried* about you. I don't think she's ever acted so concerned about one of her little worker bees before."

My entire body went taught as Satella continued on. She didn't look worried about my health. Instead, her voice was filled with drawn out syllables.

"She asked me to check on you and bring you medicine to make sure you healed quickly," Satella continued. "I thought you must've been on your deathbed with the way the old lady was acting, so I rushed straight to your room. Either you were too ill to answer my pounding on your door, or you weren't where I was told you'd be."

My eyes widened. I didn't know if lying to the vampire was the right choice. Something told me that anything short of the truth would've been an obvious lie. I couldn't tell her what happened, not when my life at Ethlow was at risk. A lie was the only choice.

"I..." My voice quickly fell off. I couldn't lie to her either, not when she had been so nice and welcoming.

"Don't worry. I told Malse that I brought you soup, and you'd be feeling well enough to return to work today. I'm glad you aren't making me a complete liar." Satella smiled, but it looked a little sadistic, as if she was thrilled to have something to hold over my head. She wasn't angry, which was better than I had expected. Although the glint in her eye worried me. Maybe it would've been better if she had been angry at me.

"Why did you tell her that?" I lowered my voice. If anyone was listening to our conversation, I didn't want to give any dangerous information away.

Satella leaned in, her smirk deepening. "Because now you owe me one, and you have to tell me what you were doing yesterday. Or should I say *who* you were doing."

My mouth went dry. I had forced myself to take a long bath after I returned to my room in the dead of night. I wanted to erase any evidence of my time with Zathrian, afraid someone would smell him on me.

Satella wiggled her brows. "Oh, I'm so right. Now, tell me everything."

I bit my lower lip, looking around the room. No one appeared to be watching us, but there were too many people around. I couldn't risk telling Satella anything, especially not somewhere that was so public. I had to tell her something, because she didn't seem like the type who let things go easily. "Not here," I whispered.

Satella cooed, clapping her hands together. "This is even better than I thought."

I quickly shushed her as a few fae craned their necks to look at what someone was squealing about at the first light of day. "Don't make such a big deal out of this. It's not what you think."

"Oh, I'm sure it's exactly as I think." She pushed the bowl of soup in front of her to me. "Eat up. You look like hell, but this will give you energy to get through your work. I will see you for dinner." The vampire winked at me before leaving the table. She was practically skipping and humming down the hall.

My head fell into my hands. I had a few hours to come up with a lie that was close enough to the truth to satisfy Satella's curiosity. Otherwise, she wouldn't leave me alone until I accidentally told her more than I should.

As I opened the door to the abandoned courtyard, a frown took over my features. Aukina and Satella sat next to each other, chatting about something that had happened in the mess hall earlier.

"She thinks she can do whatever she wants because she's fae," Aukina grumbled. I wasn't used to the mermaid looking upset.

She normally had a genuine smile plastered on her face. "I don't understand what everyone's obsession with fae is. They have magic and are immortal. They're not the only ones like that."

"They are also known for their beauty." Satella inspected her nails closely. They were painted a deep red color that sparkled as the sun hit them.

"So are vampires. You are drop-dead gorgeous," Aukina said.

"Ew. Don't say that." Satella wrinkled her nose, as if what Aukina had said was an utter lie. It was strange to see the vampire deny her beauty. Her skin was perfect, and her body was everything the village boys dreamed about back in Narthington. I didn't realize even pretty women had self-esteem issues.

"Shush," Aukina said, waving off the vampire. "You could get anyone you wanted with your looks alone. Plus, you are immortal."

"I don't have magic," Satella said.

"Yeah, but Nyri does, and she doesn't go around flaunting it," Aukina said. "I don't get why Tiafel has to act like she's better than everyone."

"What?" I let go of the door, and it slammed shut. If Aukina and Satella hadn't noticed me before, they knew I was there now.

"Aukina is upset because Tiafel insulted her food. Don't mind her." Satella leaned back, taking in the small patch of sun peeking through the roof of the buildings nearby.

"I don't have magic," I said. Normally, I would've been interested in whatever drama had happened earlier, but I was too focused on Aukina's statement.

Aukina furrowed her brows as she stared up at me. She stuck to the shadows, unlike Satella. "Aren't you a witch?"

"I'm a human." Just a simple, pathetic human. Nothing more.

"Witches can be any race." Satella inhaled deeply through her nose. "You reek of magic."

I turned my head and sniffed my shoulder. I didn't smell anything, but I didn't know what magic smelled like. "I don't have any magic," I repeated. I would've known if I had some sort of power.

Aukina pressed her lips together. She looked me up and down before inhaling deeply. "Satella's right. You have a fairly strong smell of magic on you. Is no one in your family a witch? Normally, magic is genetic."

I shook my head. "Not that I know of." I slid to the ground next to Aukina. If my parents had magic, they never used it.

"You should go see Tareen, the librarian," Satella said. "She would either know more about magic suddenly showing up in a bloodline, or she would know a book you can read to find out more."

"There's a library here?" I asked. My father had taught me to read when I was younger to help with the family finances. I hadn't been able to read for pleasure often, but when I managed to get free time, I went to the local library to read about gardening and plants.

Aukina nodded. "It's open to anyone, but if you damage a book, you have to face consequences. Tareen is a little quirky, and she rarely leaves the library, but she's nice. I'm sure she'd be able to tell you more about your magic. I think she's into witchy things."

THE DEMON KING'S PET

I wasn't sure I fully believed Aukina and Satella's claim about me having magic, but there was no reason for them to concoct a lie about that, either. I would have to find time to go to the library between work, the greenhouse, and secretly meeting up with the demon king.

Satella propped herself up onto her elbows. "So now it's time for you to spill about who you met up with yesterday. Please be sure to include details about if he or she was any good in bed."

Aukina's eyes widened. "Nyri met someone?" She squealed a little too loudly, her excitement concerning me. I hadn't planned on telling anyone other than Satella, but it was too late.

"It's not a big deal." I pulled my knees into my chest and rested my hands on my knees. My stomach made it difficult to fully wrap my arms around my legs.

Aukina leaned in closer. "You've been here for a blink of an eye, and you have already found someone to sneak away with. I'm *so* jealous. You have to tell me everything, so I can live vicariously through you."

"It's not a big deal. I don't even know if it means anything." It was a secret fling with the demon king, but nothing else had been established. "He and I agreed not to tell anyone about us."

"He?" Satella repeated. "Why can't you tell us who this *he* is? He's not trying to keep you a secret, is he? Because if he's too embarrassed to show you off—"

"No," I quickly interrupted before Satella got too heated. "If I tell you, it could get us both in trouble. He's not allowed to date anyone." None of it was a lie exactly. I hoped it'd be enough to satisfy the vampire's curiosity.

Satella hummed, debating if she liked my answer or not.

"Oh, is it one of the guardsmen?" Aukina asked. "Reamann told me they are encouraged not to date, since they have dangerous positions."

"You know Reamann?" I asked to avoid answering her question.

Aukina pursed her lips. "Unfortunately. He's always coming to the kitchen. I swear that man has an insatiable appetite, and he's always asking for seafood."

"He seemed nice enough when I met him," I said.

"She doesn't know how to handle attention," Satella said. "Now, are you going to tell us how good this mystery man is in bed, or am I going to have to threaten you?" She lifted her sharp nails up, as if to use them as a warning, but the more time I spent with Satella, the more harmless she seemed.

"Who's to say we did anything?" I wasn't used to talking about intimate things with other people. I told no one about my tangle with the farm boy. The only person I felt comfortable enough to talk to about that was Harlan, but I wasn't about to talk to my younger brother about my sexual encounter.

Satella rolled her eyes. "I saw you this morning. I am more than familiar with what the source of your exhaustion was. Now spill."

I pull my lips between my teeth, thinking about what to say without giving anything away. Any details about horns and tails were off limits. That much was obvious. "What do you want to know?"

Aukina leaned in. She wasn't pushy like Satella, but she was as curious as the vampire. "Did he make you..." She wiggled her eyebrows to imply what she was talking about.

I bit my lip in an attempt to try to hide my smile. I nodded, feeling giddy as I thought about the way Zathrian touched me. He took his time learning my body, and he knew how to touch me right. It wasn't about his pleasure—which was the only thing I thought men cared about. Maybe demons were different than humans.

"How many times?" Satella asked.

"Satella!" Aukina hit the vampire's arm. "We shouldn't pry too much."

Satella hit her back. "You're as curious as I am. I know in the five years you've been here, you haven't gotten any."

"I'm working on it." Aukina scrunched her nose.

"With that boy who delivers the supplies for the kitchen? He doesn't even know you exist." Satella's face tightened.

Aukina took a labored breath, as if they had had this conversation a hundred times. It was warming to see the way Aukina and Satella interacted with each other. They were close in a way that was new to me.

"He knows who I am. I sign for the deliveries every time," Aukina said.

"Doesn't mean he sees you. He's a stupid boy. You deserve a man, someone like—"

"Don't say it," Aukina interrupted.

"You guys are lucky," I said. Aukina and Satella redirected their attention to me, confused by my sudden statement. I scratched the back of my head, embarrassed by my outburst. "It's nice that you two have each other. I've never had a close friend like that, other than my brother, but that was different."

Aukina's face softened. She grabbed my hand and squeezed lightly. "You have us now."

My chest fluttered. It had felt like Satella and Aukina had adopted me, but I didn't know if they had felt the same. I didn't know how lonely I had felt back at home until I had people at Ethlow whom I looked forward to talking to each day. Between them and Zathrian, I could see a happy future at Ethlow. I hoped my secrets wouldn't ruin everything.

Chapter
14

I lugged a piece of broken glass that was nearly as big as me towards the door. I was determined to clean up the greenhouse to make it usable. If I figured out how to fix the cracks in the ceiling and patch the pieces of glass that had fallen out of panels, I could create a humid, warm environment all year around. If I could manage that, maybe I could figure out a way to get my hands on the seed of a bleeding heart lily. It was an outlandish goal, one I had only dreamed of as a child, but Ethlow felt different than the rest of the world. It felt like a place where things could be different and dreams were possible.

I wanted to laugh at myself. Back in Narthington, rumors of Ethlow spread among the townsfolk. Every detail about the demon estate described horrors. Anyone who went to Ethlow never returned. That was one of the last things Harlan had said to me. I had imagined a place where demons feasted on humans, which was why they never left. That wasn't true. Ethlow was a second chance for beings. If no one left, it was by choice. I couldn't imagine going back to Narthington when life at Ethlow had already given me things I had never thought were in the cards for me.

"Careful," Zathrian said. His sudden appearance didn't surprise me. I had been waiting for him to show up. We agreed that we couldn't afford any rendezvous in his room. It was too dangerous between Viridian coming and going as necessary as well as various workers coming to attend to his room. The greenhouse was the safer choice. It had been abandoned for decades. Many residents had forgotten about its existence altogether.

"I got it," I said, grunting as I tugged on the heavy piece of glass. I had already dragged it halfway to the door, so I knew I could handle it on my own.

Zathrian grabbed the hunk of glass with a single hand. I stepped back as he carried it to the door and chucked it outside in a fraction of the time it took me to get halfway across the room.

He was wearing a nice suit, one that looked too expensive to do physical labor in. He had barely used any energy to move something that had me sweating already.

"You shouldn't move glass on your own, especially not broken glass. You could've cut yourself." Zathrian brushed the dirt off his hands as he walked back to me.

I placed my hands on my hips. I appreciated his help, but I didn't want him to see me as helpless. "I was being careful. Besides, if I want to get this place cleaned up, I have to do what I can. You're not always going to be able to sneak away to help me."

"You're serious about getting this place in working condition, aren't you?" The demon king seemed a little surprised. When he dragged me here the first day, he hadn't realized he had opened up a new world for me.

I walked over to a shriveled vine, stroking the dead leaves with my fingers. "I like gardening. It feels good to plant things that can be useful for others. I want to plant an herb garden for Satella to use in her medicine, and I could grow fruit during the off seasons for Aukina, so she isn't limited by the seasons for her cooking. I also want to—" I stopped talking.

Zathrian stood behind me, his warmth wrapping around my back. Despite it being early spring, the weather at Ethlow was refusing to warm up. "You want to..." he prompted.

"It's silly," I said. I dropped the dead vine. I didn't know why I was hesitant to talk about my own dream.

"Tell me."

I bit my lip, wondering what he would say. "I want to grow bleeding heart lilies here. I don't know if it'll ever be possible. There's no way I could afford a seed for something like that, not on the small stipend I receive. Not to mention, the flowers are delicate, and even the best gardeners struggle to make them bloom. But ever since I was a little girl, I wanted to know what it was like to cultivate life like that."

Zathrian ran his fingers through my hair. His hand continued moving down my back until it rested on my hip. He pulled my back flushed against his torso. The simple gesture was enough to make my core throb with desire.

With his other hand, he pushed the hair away from my ear and leaned forward to whisper in my ear. "And where can one find bleeding heart lilies?"

My heart thundered, making it difficult to focus with the demon king's breath in my ear. My mind threatened to stop. "I've heard they can be found on the islands below the southern part of the continent. The Nescen Islands once grew them, but I also heard they died out because of a freak ice storm."

Zathrian moved his hand from my hip to my stomach, slowly moving up until he cupped my breast. He squeezed, eliciting a soft moan from me. "These flowers sound extremely rare."

I closed my eyes and leaned against his strong torso. "And expensive. Even if I could afford a seed, it probably wouldn't be worth spending the coin. I'd likely kill it, wasting a precious seed."

"I think you could do it," Zathrian said. He slipped his hand under my shirt, returning it to my chest. He lightly pinched my nipple, making my back arch with pleasure. I pressed my butt into his crotch and felt his hardness pressing against me.

"You know nothing about my gardening skills." My breath increased as Zathrian continued playing with my body.

"The seeds you planted by the house are thriving. That's enough for me to have faith in your skills." He nipped my ear, sending a tingle down my spine.

I was surprised those seeds were growing, since I hadn't checked on them since planting them. After discovering the greenhouse, it had become my priority. "It's not like I'll ever get the chance to grow a bleeding heart lily. Even if I managed to find one, I don't have any money."

"You never know," he murmured against my neck. He sucked and nipped my sensitive skin, making it difficult to focus on anything else.

I spun around, needing to touch him.

I moved my hand between his legs and palmed him over his pants.

"Nyri," he moaned, spurring my actions even more.

I fiddled with his pants, struggling to free him. My hands shook with nerves and excitement. When I finally freed him, he sprang free. I looked at his throbbing cock. I wrapped my fingers over the base, earning another groan. I wanted to make Zathrian feel good, like he had done to me countless times.

I moved my hand, watching his face closely to make sure he liked what I was doing. His eyes fluttered shut as I moved my hand back and forth, but it wasn't enough. I dropped to my knees, and his eyes snapped open.

"What are you doing?" He licked his lips, watching my every movement,

"Making you feel good," I said, determined to follow through with my claim. I wasn't skilled in the bedroom like Zathrian was, but I could learn with practice.

I leaned forward and wrapped my lips around the tip of his cock. He muttered in a language I didn't understand and twitched under my touch. I took a little more of him in my mouth, but I knew I'd never fit the whole thing in. His size was intimidating as I stared directly at it, but I wasn't going to back down from the challenge. I flicked my tongue over his tip, and a salty taste filled my mouth. I repeated the motion, and this time Zathrian twisted his fingers in my hair.

He rolled his neck, his face tight. I took a little more of him in my mouth, and his grip on my hair tightened. I moved my hand from the base of his cock up to meet my mouth. Between my mouth and hand, I stroked every part of his length, slowly picking up the pace as he twitched with pleasure.

I slowed after several moments, getting tired, but Zathrian's eyes snapped open. "Don't stop." His words bordered between a command and a plea. The desperation made my core throb. Knowing I was the one making him break his commanding aura sent pleasure between my legs. I wanted him to cry out my name the way I had cried out his many times.

I pushed myself to take him even deeper, stretching my jaw to fit as much of him in my mouth. When he hit the back of my throat, I coughed. He quickly pulled out of my mouth, worry replacing his pleasure.

"Don't stop," I said before he could ask if I was okay. I was determined to make him come.

Zathrian tightened his grip, my order driving him mad. He pushed his cock between my lips again, sliding deep into my mouth. I used my hand to pump the base of his cock as he used my mouth to pleasure himself. He looked at my eyes as his cock moved between my lips.

"I love your pretty little mouth wrapped around me," he muttered.

I groaned against him, and the reverberation made him moan loudly. The spot between my legs was slick with desire. I wanted Zathrian inside of me desperately, but I was more determined to continue sucking him off until he couldn't take anymore.

Zathrian's tail moved between my legs, as if he saw my desire in my eyes and wanted to return the favor. His tail slid into my pants, going straight for my entrance. I lost my rhythm as he pumped in and out of me, but he held my head firmly as he thrusted. There was no stopping either of us. We were too wrapped up in the pleasure of each other.

I loved having both ends of me filled with him, knowing he was feeling the same pleasure as me. It felt different than his cock being between my legs. It was messier and more thrilling. He picked up his pace, fucking my face faster while thrusting his tail harder. My orgasm hit me out of nowhere, and my body convulsed around both his tail and cock. That sensation pushed him over the edge, and he filled my mouth with his seed, not stopping until every last drop went down my throat.

When he stopped, he lifted me off the ground and pulled me into a kiss, not caring that his taste lingered in my mouth. "You are incredible," he whispered, his lips brushing against mine. "I don't know if I'll ever be able to stay away from you."

I lifted onto my toes to kiss him again. I felt the same way, but it seemed dangerous to say out loud, as if it'd jinx everything. When we broke the kiss, I rested my head against his chest, wanting to memorize every second I had with him. There was a knot in the pit of my stomach, terrified that our time together was already running out. I didn't understand the sudden fear, but I couldn't push it away.

I pulled away from him and turned back to the dead vine, wondering how long it would take to turn this place around and if I had enough time to accomplish everything I wanted to. I paused, leaning in to look at the plant closer. It almost looked green, but I must've been imagining it. It was dead when I looked at it before.

"Do you sense magic coming from me?" I asked, blinking several times. The question came from nowhere, but I hadn't been able to get the conversation with Aukina and Satella out of my head.

"Yes." Zathrian spoke as if it was the most obvious thing in the world.

I slowly turned towards him. "I didn't know I had magic, but my friends told me the other day. I thought maybe it was a joke." There was no way three separate people said they sensed magic from me out of jest, but I couldn't wrap my head around the idea of having magic.

Zathrian pushed a piece of my hair out of my face. "You didn't know?" I shook my head. "I'm surprised. I saw it in your aura. I assumed you knew with how strong it is."

I pressed my lips together. How could I have gone twenty-five years through life without anyone mentioning my magic before. "Do you know what kind of magic it is?"

"No. That's not as easy to sense, but maybe the librarian can help you."

I nodded slowly. "Yeah, that's what my friends said."

"You could talk to her tomorrow." Zathrian's face tightened. "I won't be able to sneak away to see you for a few days. Another demon king is coming to visit, so I won't get a moment alone."

I ignored the tightening in my chest. I hadn't known Zathrian for long. I could stand a couple of days away from him, especially knowing why I wouldn't see him this time. "One of the five demon rulers?" I asked. I didn't know much about the other kingdoms other than there was a demon on the throne, appointed to rule over and protect the land given to them.

"Yes. It's best you stay away from my part of the estate, no matter what anyone else tells you. Our visitor isn't like me. He's not fond of humans." Zathrian's voice was tight. If Zathrian—a demon—thought the visitor was bad news, I didn't want to ever set sights on the other demon ruler.

"I will make sure to spend my free time in the library and stay out of trouble," I announced. It was the perfect opportunity to do some research.

Chapter
15

The library was bigger than I had imagined. The walls stretched several stories high with platforms wrapping around every level to provide access to the books. Ladders were placed against the walls at intervals, giving access to the different levels. My throat tightened at the thought of climbing higher. I had never been off the ground that high, and I wasn't interested in finding out what it felt like.

There was no one around, and my footsteps echoed in the empty air. It was beautiful, but a little eerie. I had thought everyone loved books, but not here. I continued moving deeper, glancing at the stacks and stacks of bookcases on the first floor. I had no idea where to begin. I had never been in a place with a fraction of the books collected here. The library at Narthington only had a few shelves in total.

"Hello?" I winced as my voice bounced around the room. It felt wrong to be that loud in a library.

A clash echoed back at me, followed by a yelp. I moved, looking for the source of the cry, but there were too many stacks blocking the view of the other side of the room.

"Are you okay?" I asked.

"Coming!" a shrill voice boomed back. Various concerning noises thudded from the unknown location followed by silence.

I chewed on my inner cheek, unsure if I should continue to search for the body that belonged to the voice or if I should wait for her to find me. A moment later, a soft whiz filled the air. A breeze hit my face, and then I saw a woman dressed in black sitting on a stick, flying directly towards me. Her brown curly hair flew wildly behind her, and her skirt rode dangerously high on her thighs. Her dark brown eyes were big, bordering on the size of a doll's. She had a wild gaze in those eyes as she flew directly towards me.

I yelped, ducking in time to miss a collision. The woman yelped again, and a crash filled my ears. She ran into a stack of books on the table, knocking everything down. I rushed over to her side and offered her my hand.

"Are you okay?"

She cackled, pressing her hand on her plush stomach. A snort turned into a wheeze, leaving me more concerned than before. I crouched down, unsure of what to do.

"Should I call the healer?"

The woman calmed her breathing and sat up, her hair all over the place. "It's a disease of the lungs. Satella has already looked at me. It's nothing she can heal, but she gives me treatments that help. You're awfully kind for asking."

My heart hammered in my chest, stressed from the concern over the woman, but she acted like she was completely fine. "What was that thing you were flying on?"

She reached over and grabbed the large stick she had been on a moment prior. It branched off at the front into three prongs that curled around in a decorative nature. "It's an old coat rack. No one uses it, so I thought I'd experiment flying on it. It worked okay, but brooms are more aerodynamic." She crinkled her button nose at that statement, as if she hated the idea of flying on a broom.

She pushed herself off the ground, but between the books and the broken table, she struggled. I offered her my hand. "Let me help you up."

Together, we got her onto her feet. Now that she wasn't flying through the air, I was surprised at how short and round she was. She looked cute and squishable, especially her freckled cheeks.

She brushed her dress off. It was all black, hugging her curves in a way that made them look beautiful. When she was done, she reached her hand out. "I'm Tareen, the librarian, local witch, and interested in all things black." She chuckled. "That last one was a joke. I swear I don't only have black in my closet."

I laughed, unsure of how else to act. "I'm Nyri. I'm new here."

Tareen stopped laughing, but a soft smile was left on her lips. "Let me guess. You were born in a human town that associates magic with demons and death, so when you came into your magic, you were ousted from the community and forced to go to the only place that could accept someone like you?"

"No," I said slowly, unsure of how else to respond.

"Oh, that must be my story." She laughed again, but this time, I didn't laugh with her.

"I actually didn't know I had magic until recently." I looked away from her eyes, not wanting to let the librarian see the shame in mine. Everyone acted surprised I didn't know I had magic, as if it was the most obvious thing in the world.

Tareen pressed a finger against her cheek and leaned in. She waved her other hand in front of me, curling her fingers in a delicate manner. "Your magic is new. How long did you say you've been here?"

"About a fortnight."

She stepped closer, and I resisted the urge to step away. Her eyes scanned me as if I was an enigma. "Strange." She stepped back and walked away.

I followed her, unsure if I wanted to wait for her to return. "What's strange?"

"All magic has a personality. You can tell if it's playful or serious—that kind of thing. You can also tell when magic is new or old. It takes some practice and exposure, but when you start paying attention, you learn to understand others' magic." She walked through bookcases, occasionally grabbing a book as she moved. It was hard to keep up with her quick pace and erratic path. "What's strange is your magic is like a baby fawn, one that's less than two weeks old."

She stopped and pointed at a shelf too high for her to grab. "Take that book." I did as she asked, but she didn't bother to take it from me before she continued on. "How old are you?"

"Twenty-five." I tried not to wince as I said it. I knew it wasn't old, but my mother always made me feel like I was on the verge of death, since I hadn't found a spouse to take care of me.

"Interesting." She grabbed two books and shoved them into my hands. "Was anyone in your family a witch?"

"Not that I know of."

"What's your last name?"

"Chamire."

"Interesting. Very interesting."

I didn't understand what was going on. The questions Tareen asked seemed to matter, but I didn't know why. She didn't bother explaining as she weaved in and out of bookshelves. She grabbed one last book, one that was thicker and larger than the rest. We left the shelves, and the librarian dropped the pile of books on a table.

She flipped through the largest book until she found a page. She used her finger to scan the words. "Ah hah!"

"What?" I still held the books she gave me, waiting for instructions on what to do with them.

"Beala Chamire was born in Aphelon. She was one of the greatest witches in her town. She had a daughter, but she disappeared. There's no other information on her." Tareen looked up at me. "Do you know her?"

The name was vaguely familiar. My mother had spoken it a long time ago, but she made a point not to talk about the woman who gave birth to her. "That's my grandmother, I think."

Tareen pointed to the books in my hands. "What are you doing? Set those down."

I did as told. "What does this mean?"

"That you don't take initiative," Tareen said. "Those books were heavy. Why didn't you set them down?"

I pursed my lips. The witch's mind seemed to go all over the place. "No, I mean about Beala."

"It means you didn't suddenly develop magic from nowhere, which means you're not a miracle case. You're simply a human from a long line of powerful witches. I don't know why your magic didn't show up sooner. I'd love to talk to your mother about that."

I looked away, anger flaring in my chest. Not only had my mother kicked me out when I wasn't of use to her, but she kept my true heritage a secret from me. "Good luck with that. She's the one who kicked me out of my home."

"Oh." A thick silence filled the air. Tareen clicked her tongue. "Well, if you have any questions about magic or your heritage, these books should have any information you need. Good luck!" She left before I had a chance to ask her more questions. I wasn't sure if it was a good or bad thing yet.

I stared at the pile of books, not sure where to begin. I plopped into the chair, overwhelmed by the mess in front of me. I opened the first one and dove in, knowing it was the only way I'd find any information.

After hours of flipping through books, I felt no closer to understanding my magic than before. I couldn't understand half of the words I read, since they were outside the realm of my education. Not only that, but the information I did understand was conflicting and confusing. Some people were born able to use their magic. Some gained it at a specific age—there didn't appear to be guidelines defining why either happened. Some magic was as natural as breathing, but there was also magic that could be learned by non-magic users through the use of spells and herbs. Then there were seances, cleanses, exorcisms.

None of it explained why my magic had awakened because of my arrival at Ethlow. None of it explained why my mother had kept a massive secret from me. None of it told me where to go or how to use my magic.

I closed the book in front of me, knowing my brain wouldn't be able to absorb any other information I managed to shift through—not tonight. I closed my eyes and leaned back, trying to straighten the kink in my back that had begun to develop over an hour ago.

Clink. The sound came from the other side of the library. I hadn't heard Tareen since I sat down with the books. *Clink. Clink.* It didn't sound like Tareen.

I followed the strange clicking noise until I stood at the other end of the library where several windows looked out into the backyard. *Clink.* The sound was coming from the farthest window. I approached slowly, unsure of what to make of the noise. When I reached the window, I paused. A crow stood on the little ledge on the outside. There was something silver in its beak that he used to hit the glass with. I took a step closer to get a better look.

The crow stopped and looked at me. Its beady black eyes met mine, and it tilted its head. Suddenly, it dropped the silver item and flew away, making me jump. I rushed to the window and watched it fly toward the roof, where it disappeared into a larger shadow that looked like it belonged to a person. I rubbed my eyes, and when I opened them again, there was nothing there.

The sun was gone, making me realize how late it was. My eyes were tired after hours of attempting to read books. My mind must have created images out of shadows in my tired state.

The silver item sat on the other side of the window. With some effort, I pushed the glass up. Once it was cracked enough, I slipped my hand to the other side and picked up the item the bird had been holding. It was a small metal ring with a red gem in the center of it. It was well crafted and looked like it'd cost a bag of coins.

I slipped it into my pocket, not wanting to leave the trinket outside. I shoved the window back in place, deciding it was time for bed. I looked for Tareen as I moved through the library, but the place was eerily quiet. The lamps that had kept the room bright had dimmed, and shadows crawled around every corner.

My heart thumped, a feeling of unease sinking into my bones. It felt like someone or something was watching me, but I didn't hear anything. In fact, the pure silence made my skin crawl. The usual hums and creaks of the building were gone.

I was imagining it. It was late, and I had been reading about strange things. My mind was creating something out of nothing.

I walked faster, eager to return to my room for the night, but then a creak from behind made me pause. I looked over my shoulder. "Tareen?" I called quietly, hoping the witch would appear in that dramatic manner of hers. There was nothing.

I turned back around, on the verge of running back to my room, but a large figure blocked my path. He was as tall as Zathrian, and large horns curled out of his head. Dark spikes covered the horns, the kind that could tear my hands open if I touched them. His eyes glowed red, and a mouth full of sharp teeth smiled at me.

"My, my. I wasn't expecting to find a little mouse here," he said. His voice was deep and smooth, surprisingly kind to the ears compared to his vicious appearance.

Run!

A scream twisted at the base of my throat, desperate to come out. I forced it down, not wanting to look afraid. Acting afraid gave a predator more reasons to attack.

"Excuse me. I have somewhere to be." I stepped to the side to walk past him.

He grabbed my arm, digging his sharp claws into my skin. "We just met. It's rude to run away, little mouse."

Chapter 16

I struggled to free myself, but he dug his claws deeper into my skin. There was nothing I could do to free myself from the demon. I was at his mercy, and it terrified me. "Let me go." My voice shook, giving away how afraid I was.

His smile broadened, flashing his sharp teeth in the moonlight, peeking through the windows. "You are more of a fighter than I expected, little mouse. Humans usually piss themselves at the sight of me alone. You're scared, yes, but it's not the same."

My body shook. I couldn't use physical strength to free myself, and there was no one around to help me. There was only one way I'd get out of the situation alive.

"Someone is waiting for me. They'll know if I don't show up." If he thought someone was expecting me, maybe he'd let me go.

He pulled me closer, bringing his face only inches away from mine. "Nice try, but I can practically taste the lie on your tongue." He leaned in more, and I twisted my head away as much as I could. He dragged his tongue up my neck until his mouth was at my ear. A cry of disgust and terror escaped my throat. "So delicious," he whispered. "There's no use fighting. Even if you weren't lying about someone waiting for you, it wouldn't matter. I am a demon king. I am untouchable, which means I can do whatever I want to little mice like you."

The blood in my face drained. Zathrian warned me to avoid going near his part of the estate because he was afraid I'd run into the demon king guest. I thought I was safe in the library, but I was wrong.

"Who are you?" I asked. It was clear I wouldn't outsmart him, but if I delayed him long enough, maybe Tareen would return and get help.

He clicked his tongue. "You should know better, human. I am one of the great rulers of these five lands. Everyone who knows what's good for them would know that I am the greatest of the five kings, King Jathral."

"I never went to school," I said. It wasn't a lie. My parents taught me everything I knew, but they never talked about the other demon kings. They rarely talked about Zathrian, the king of Kinzlea, our own homeland.

"Shame. Maybe I should teach you a few things." He ran his claws down my neck hard enough to remind me how easy it'd be for him to slit my throat, but not hard enough to leave a mark. "If you make a pact with me, I can teach you whatever you wish to know."

I looked up at him, hating every second he touched me. "I would never make a pact with a demon, especially not one as disgusting as you."

He hissed as he grabbed a fist full of my hair, yanking my head back. I cried out as pain shocked my body.

"I was trying to be nice. I'll take whatever I want from you either way. If you hadn't been stupid enough to reject me, at least you could've had something in return." Jathral let go of my arm and dragged me away by my hair.

I grabbed his wrist, trying to lessen the pain. "Let me go!" I screamed as loudly as possible. I didn't know if anyone would hear me, but there was no point in staying quiet. Out of the corner of my eyes, I saw a red flash come from my pocket, but Jathral twisted his hands in my hair, making it impossible to think about anything other than the pain.

"I'm not letting you go anytime soon." He yanked harder, making me lose my balance. He didn't care as he dragged me like a rag doll. Tears streamed down my face, fearing this was the end. I closed my eyes, wishing I had a little longer, a few more hours with Zathrian.

A roar echoed through the library, so loud books vibrated off the shelves and fell to the floor. King Jathral stopped, but he didn't let go of me.

"Oh, there you are Zath," King Jathral said. "I lost track of you, and thought I might find you here. Instead, I found a little mouse. Isn't she darling?" He lifted me up by the hair until I dangled in the air.

Zathrian's eyes flashed the moment he saw my face. His skin darkened to a deep red. Gold tattoos glimmered against the red, and his muscles rippled, growing bigger. He spread out his wings, which now had little spikes running along the bones. He towered over Jathral, sharp teeth replacing the incisors that I was used to.

I hadn't seen his true demon form before—not even close.

"Let. Her. Go." Zathrian's voice was twisted with rage, sounding nothing like the demon I had come to know.

Jathral pulled me closer, finally letting my feet touch the ground. "Oh, I wasn't aware this human belonged to you. Usually demons mark their pets." He leaned in and dragged his nose over my neck. I tried to squirm away from him, but it was pointless. "Now that I think about it, she does smell like you."

Zathrian roared again, his power wrapping around my chest. I knew he was strong, but I hadn't known his power was that intense. If his magic was directed at me, it could make my heart stop without a single touch.

"If you hurt her—"

"You'll what?" Jathral taunted. "You don't own her. She holds none of your protections against other demons. If I kill her or take her to be my slave, your claims on her wouldn't hold up against the council, as you fully know. If you cared about her, you should've marked her. Oh, wait." A soft chuckle filled the air. This was all a game to him.

"Let her go now, or I will tear you into a million pieces." Zathrian's eyes glowed, and his teeth extended. Terror filled my chest.

King Jathral wrapped his fingers around my throat and tightened his grip, cutting off any air. I clawed at his hand as my lungs ached.

"It's a shame how fragile humans are. Before you reach me, she will be dead, like your precious Leira." Jathral tightened his grip, and the edge of my vision darkened. I continued fighting against him, but I was growing weaker by the second. I was going to die. I felt it watching me from the shadows, waiting to take me to the netherworld.

"Please." The word was broken as it slipped past Zathrian's lips. He looked at me, pain etched into his face. He looked helpless. We were both at Jathral's mercy.

I focused on his glowing yellow eyes in an attempt to stay conscious. The rest of him had twisted and changed in his fury, but his eyes were still the sun. If I was going to die, I wanted Zathrian's eyes to be the last thing I saw.

"Is the great King Zathrian begging?" Jathral chuckled, as if he had been craving this moment.

Zathrian stepped forward. "What do you want?"

"I want—"

"Let go of that woman right now." Viridian's voice cut through the air.

"Master," Jathral whispered, his voice going quiet.

Viridian stepped out of the shadows. Black fire covered every inch of his body. "I said let her go. She is a resident of Ethlow, which means she is under the king of Kinzlea's protection. Any harm that comes to her will be taken as a personal offense against King Zathrian's territory." The fire around Viridian burst, covering the room in shadows.

Or maybe I was losing consciousness.

Jathral released my neck, and I collapsed to the floor. I felt like I was going to lose consciousness, but then another flash of red gave me a small surge of energy.

"A simple misunderstanding. I'm sure this doesn't need to be turned into anything more, right?" Jathral made his voice smooth and calm, acting the role of an innocent perfectly.

"Leave," Viridian roared.

Jathral grimaced, but he didn't say anything else as he strode out of the library.

I pressed my palms to the ground and focused on taking slow breaths, fighting against the unconsciousness that threatened to take over. My throat burned, and my arm was covered in blood from Jathral's nails. I couldn't stop shaking, knowing how close to death I had come. I was too focused on trying not to cry that I didn't hear Zathrian approach.

He dropped to his knees in front of me and pulled me into his chest. Viridian's eyes burned into us, and I wanted to tell Zathrian to stop, because it'd only make it worse, but I couldn't find the words. I wanted to lean into Zathrian's touch after the way Jathral had threatened me.

Heavy footsteps approached, and I didn't dare look up, afraid to see the look on the master's face.

"You need to leave, too, sire." Viridian's voice was colder than ice. Though Zathrian was the king, Viridian spoke as if he was in control.

Zathrian clung to me. "I can't leave her."

I peeked at Viridian. There was no sympathy on his face. It was as if he was carved from stone.

"You don't have a choice."

Zathrian didn't move. Instead, he stroked the back of my head, soothing the pain from my hair being pulled.

Viridian stepped closer, and I winced, afraid of what the demon would do. Jathral had shown me how cruel demons could be, and I didn't want to experience it again.

"I swear to you, I will not let harm come to her while she's in my care. Leave now, and we'll discuss this later." No sympathy, but there was something else hidden beneath the surface of the master of the house. I would've guessed concern, but after his threats to me, I couldn't believe that.

Zathrian's grip loosened. I clenched his shirt, panic rising in my throat, but I couldn't speak. It hurt to try. He cupped my cheek and pressed his lips against my forehead. "I'm sorry," he muttered before lowering me to the ground.

Something inside of me cracked as Zathrian stood. He walked away, and I wanted to run after him, but my body shook too violently to have control over it.

Only after Zathrian was out of sight, Viridian moved closer to me. He let out a long sigh. "I knew you were going to be trouble the moment you showed up at our door." He scooped me into his arms, picking me up with ease.

I opened my mouth, ready to defend myself, but the noise that came out was a raspy groan, resembling nothing like words.

"Don't speak. You'll make the injury worse. Your windpipe was crushed." His voice was flat. No sympathy. Just facts.

I tried to focus on breathing, but it hurt. Everything hurt, even my heart. Zathrian and I barely had time together. If we never saw each other again, it shouldn't have mattered, but the thought broke my heart. I feared what would happen. He may not have caught us together, but the possessive way Zathrian reacted to Jathral made it obvious. The master of the house knew we had broken the third rule of Ethlow.

I barely noticed when Viridian stopped in front of the healer's room. He kicked the door, making it fly open with ease.

A shout of surprise echoed from deep in the room. "Holy hell. Haven't you ever heard of knocking?" Satella's voice grew louder. "I could've been in the middle of—" She cut her voice off the second she saw Viridian. "Holy hell. What happened to her?"

"Where can I put her?" he asked, ignoring the healer's question.

Satella rushed to put a sheet on a small bed in the corner of the room. Viridian set me down gently.

"What happened?" Satella asked as she scanned my body, her face lingering on the blood soaking my arm.

"Her windpipe was crushed. That is the worst injury. The wounds on her arm are deep, but they didn't pierce anything vital. Make sure she wasn't poisoned. I don't think any of her bones were broken, but you should double-check. I trust you will treat her until she's healthy. Don't ask questions. They won't be answered." He made eye contact with me, a silent threat. If I spoke about what happened, it'd only get me in more trouble than I was already in.

Satella opened her mouth, a million questions burning her tongue, but she decided not to ask any of them. "I will take care of her."

"Good." He left without another word, leaving Satella to patch me up.

She cleaned the cuts on my arm first, put on a salve that burned, and then wrapped the wounds. She checked the rest of my body, putting on a mix of oils and salves as she found various injuries. She didn't speak as she worked. Her lips pressed into a tight line as she focused on her job. The last thing she did was boil water and add a slew of ingredients to a cup.

She gently pressed the cup into my hands, keeping her hands on top of mine to make sure I didn't drop it. "Drink slowly."

The first sip I took instantly made me cough. The mixture was a potent level of bitter herbs. It stung my throat and left a thick coating on my tongue.

"I know," she whispered, slowly lowering the cup. "I want to ask you what happened, but I know you can't speak about it, for more reasons than one."

Tears bubbled in my eyes. I had never been that terrified in my life, but watching Zathrian walk away from me hurt worse than all of my injuries combined. I couldn't stop the tears from coming out of my eyes. If I could use my voice, I didn't know what I would say to her. How could I tell her that I had fallen for the demon king, whom I barely knew, and now it was all ruined?

Satella pulled me into her, holding my head against her chest. I didn't know how long she held me like that while I cried, but her touch was healing in a way I had never experienced. Despite the hollowness in my chest, at least I knew I wasn't alone with the healer by my side.

Chapter
17

I fell in and out of consciousness for days. My injuries weren't bad enough to keep me unconscious, especially with Satella's healing touch, but there was a heaviness in my chest that made it difficult to keep my eyes open. The future felt grim. I wasn't sure if I'd see Zathrian again, and now that Viridian knew we had broken the rules, I'd likely be kicked out of the place I had started to see as a home.

A soft knock at the door pulled me out of a wave of unconsciousness, but I couldn't bring myself to open my eyes.

"Is she awake?" Aukina tried to whisper, but her voice traveled easily to my ears.

"No." The worry in Satella's voice hurt.

"I baked muffins, hoping she'd be awake. Were her injuries that bad?"

Satella hesitated. "No. It's not her body that's struggling right now."

More silence made me crack my eyes open. The two were staring at each other with frowns on their faces. Both of them had dark circles under their eyes, as if they hadn't slept a wink since the attack.

"What happened?" Aukina asked.

Satella pressed her lips together and motioned for Aukina to enter the room. "I wish I knew. I was told not to ask questions."

Aukina huffed, moving over to my bed. "I know he's the master of the house, but this isn't fair. She's our friend. We deserve to know what happened." She sat down on the bed, but she didn't notice me looking at her.

"It has to do with that guy she's been seeing. I'm sure of it." Satella moved to her work bench and moved bottles around to keep her hands preoccupied.

"I asked Reamann if there were any attacks on the border, but he said it's been peaceful. Nothing has dared to come around, not while there were two demon kings on the premises. He also didn't know anyone who Nyri could have been seeing." The mermaid let out a long sigh. "I hate that I don't know what happened."

"I know." Satella pressed her hands against the wooden desk and let her head hang low. "I wish she'd wake up for longer than a few minutes, so I know she'll get through this."

Neither of them spoke for a long moment. They averted their eyes from each other, their worry filling the air. I was tired, but knowing I was causing them any kind of emotional strain was enough to keep me awake.

"Has anyone told you both that you're bad at whispering?" My voice was raw and sounded nothing like myself, but the pain was minor compared to a few days ago.

"Nyri!" Aukina squealed. She threw her arms over me and hugged me tightly. An involuntary groan slipped past my lips.

"Careful," Satella said. She floated across the room, carrying a cup of something steaming. "If you hurt my patient, I will have to hurt you."

Aukina loosened her grip, but she didn't let go. "I'm so relieved you're awake."

Satella shooed Aukina away. She helped me sit up, keeping her hand on my back. The cup was filled with the same liquid as before, and though it was hard to swallow, I didn't cough it up this time.

"Good," the healer said. "You won't be back to normal for at least another week or so, but the fact that you can talk is a good sign."

I nodded, grateful no permanent damage had been done—at least not to my body.

"So, are you going to tell us what happened or what?" Aukina asked.

I pulled my knees to my chest and looked down. If I wanted to talk about what happened, Viridian had made it painfully clear I wasn't supposed to tell anyone what happened. It wasn't against the rules, but I had a feeling Viridian's word was law. With nothing more than his voice, he made two demon kings stand down, as if he was more powerful than both of them.

Satella hissed at Aukina, shaking her head. "If you want to talk, we're here to listen, but don't do anything you don't want to."

I wasn't ready to tell them what happened. I wasn't sure that was something I'd ever be able to relive. I had too many questions about things that didn't make sense. I doubted they knew any more than I did, but I needed to try.

"Why is it against the rules to interact with the demon king?"

Aukina and Satella shared a look. Aukina raised her eyebrows as if to say, *Don't*. Satella tilted her head, her silent words screaming, *We can't hide this forever*. Aukina's chest collapsed, giving in.

Satella was the one to speak. "Every rule of Ethlow is created for the protection of the beings who seek refuge here. We all work, so no one is taken advantage of. We stay inside at night, because there are creatures who lurk outside that could kill us in ways that belong only in nightmares. We stay away from the demon king, because the last woman who got close to him was killed."

"Leira," I whispered, thinking back to Jathral's taunt.

Aukina and Satella shared a look again.

"Where did you hear that name?" Aukina asked.

I couldn't tell her that without telling her everything. "What happened to Leira?"

"I've only heard stories, since it happened before I came to Ethlow," Aukina said.

"It happened right before my arrival at Ethlow. I had never been in a place so thick with grief." Satella's voice became hollow, as if the memory of it haunted her. "Before I knew anyone, I had learned Leira's name. Everyone talked about her as if she was a saint, and I learned so many stories about a woman I could never meet. She was the sweetest person to walk the lands, according to others. She helped everyone out, never asking for anything in return. She taught others to read, the ones who never had the privilege of an education. She made desserts for every holiday—even if it wasn't one she celebrated. It was no wonder she caught the demon king's eyes. Everyone said it was love. The way she looked at him could be described as nothing less. It was a wild and rampant romance. It burned so brightly, it was no wonder it burned out so quickly.

"One day, a scream could be heard throughout the entire estate. Everyone knew it belonged to Leira, and when they went to look for her, all they could find was her blood staining the grand hall."

Satella looked down at her hands, spreading them in front of her. "No one ever really knew what happened to her. There were a thousand different rumors. Some saying the demon king snapped and killed her. Others saying she snapped under the attention of the demon king and killed herself. People started making up stories to get attention. It was impossible to guess what was true, since I hadn't been there for it. All I know is, when I showed up at Ethlow, Master Viridian had emphasized the third rule, saying anyone who interacted with the demon king would be punished. He never explained why."

"So Za—" I cut myself off, realizing I nearly said his name. "The demon king's lover got killed."

Satella nodded, making my heart squeeze. No wonder Zathrian had been cautious around me at first, saying it was dangerous to be with him. I couldn't imagine losing someone I loved. The pain Zathrian must've felt from Leira's death...

"Is the demon king the one who hurt you?" Aukina asked. She hardly moved as she waited for my answer.

"No," I said sharply. "He wouldn't do something like that." I didn't care if there had been rumors about him hurting Leira. I refused to believe Zathrian was capable of something like that.

"He's the one you've been seeing, isn't he?" Satella asked.

I pressed my lips together, unable to confirm her suspicions. By not denying it, it was confirmation enough. It didn't matter. Whatever was between us couldn't continue. Even if Zathrian wasn't the one who hurt Leira, she died, and our secret was out. "I'm not seeing anyone anymore."

I waited for the tears to come, but my chest felt hollow. All I wanted to do was see Zathrian and fall into his arms, but for once, my logic was winning. I caused trouble for Zathrian and nearly got myself killed in the process. It was better for the both of us if I stayed away. I couldn't stand the idea of putting him through that kind of pain again.

"You should be able to return to your room today," Satella chirped after doing a thorough check-up. "You could even go back to work tomorrow, but if you want, I can tell that old goblin you need a few more days."

Malse had come by to visit me the day before. She told me to get better quickly, so I would stop slacking off. Her words had been harsh, but relief had flooded her eyes when she saw I was okay. It was strange to think the strict seamstress had a golden heart.

"No. I'm ready to go back to work." Sitting in my room was the worst possible thing I could do. With Satella there, she was able to distract me when she wasn't busy. She even gave me simple work to help her. It kept my mind off the one person I tried not to think about.

"I thought you might say that," Satella chuckled. "I'm going to miss having the company. It gets lonely here sometimes."

I couldn't imagine being in the same room all day with no one around. Even though my work as a seamstress was solo work, it was comforting to listen to the idle noise of others working. It reminded me of listening to my family buzz around the home while I did my chores. For a moment, I let my mind wander to them, wondering if they were doing okay. I hoped the spring was treating them better in Narthington than it was treating us at Ethlow. I hoped Harlan had caught the eye of a young maiden and was falling in love. I hoped Melody was growing big and strong.

Noises from outside the healer's room pulled me out of my deep thoughts. At first, I couldn't understand it. Then, it was clear that someone was having an argument outside. Satella looked at the door, as curious and concerned as I was.

"I need to see her."

My body froze, clearly hearing the voice of the demon king.

"I can't let you do that, sire. It's against the rules." Viridian's voice was as icy as ever.

"I don't care. I need to see that she's okay. It's my fault she was hurt."

"Which is why I won't let you near her again. I won't let you put the young lady in danger because you can't control your emotions."

My heart thundered. They could've had the conversation anywhere. Why did it have to be where I could hear them, where Zathrian's voice opened up the void in my chest, reminding me how much I missed his touch? All I wanted to do was run to him and throw myself into his arms.

"Do you want to see him?" Satella whispered.

Yes.

"No." If I saw him, I knew it'd be nearly impossible to walk away.

"Are you sure?" She knew it was against the rules. She knew Viridian stood on the other side of the door. If she did anything, she would've received punishment from the master, something I refused to let my friend go through on my behalf.

I nodded, not trusting my words. I wanted to see Zathrian more than anything.

Satella pulled her lips tight and stood. She opened the door quickly, receiving instant silence from the two demons arguing outside the door. "If you two wish to continue arguing, I request you do it somewhere it won't disturb my healing patients." It was impressive how firm she was considering who she was speaking to.

Viridian straightened his spine, slowly turning his gaze to Satella. His eyes flashed black. I tensed, waiting for him to scold her. Instead, he said, "We were leaving. Come, sire. You have work to do."

Zathrian stepped forward, moving closer to Satella. His eyes scanned the room, determination filling them. When he spotted me, his shoulders collapsed. He stopped breathing, and so did I. There was a longing in his eyes that I knew was in mine as well, but guilt pressed his lips together, keeping him silent.

I wanted to tell him that nothing that happened was his fault. I wanted to say that it didn't change anything, but it would be a lie. I couldn't sleep at night without a sedative provided by Satella because I saw Jathral's eyes haunting me, waiting to take me away to mess with Zathrian. I didn't know what happened to Leira, but the loneliness that had been in Zathrian's eyes when I first saw him said enough. The guilt in them now said even more.

If I got hurt because of him, he'd never forgive himself. It was better we were both safe and apart than risk hurting each other by being together.

"She needs rest," Satella said. She slowly shut the door on Zathrian's face, putting an end to whatever was between us.

Chapter 18

The thought of going to the greenhouse made my chest ache. I knew the moment I stepped into the glass building, memories of everything I did with Zathrian would come flooding back. I told myself I would go back. I had already lost Zathrian. I didn't want to lose my love for gardening because of him, too.

Days passed with me telling myself I would go out to the greenhouse, yet I couldn't build the courage to leave the estate. I waited for a sign or for Viridian to approach me, telling me I had to leave Ethlow for breaking the rules, but he had been absent for days. So had Zathrian.

I found myself looking around every corner for the demon king, but I didn't know why I bothered. I had never seen him in the hallways in Ethlow. If I wanted to see him, there were two places that were my best chance. I avoided them both.

On the fourth day, a crow cawing outside the mess hall grated my nerves. It was an obnoxious sound, the bird repeatedly yapping, drawing nearly everyone's attention in the hall. I reached into my pocket where I had kept the ring since the incident. Vague memories of a red light flashing out of my pocket were burned into my brain, but I couldn't tell if they had been hallucinations from lack of oxygen or not. Now that I was healthy, the ring looked like a simple ring.

Part of me wondered if it was a bad omen. I was attacked after I saw the bird. However, it was bad luck to get rid of a gift a crow gave—at least that was what I had heard.

The cawing didn't stop, and several residents filed out to find peace somewhere else. I found myself staring out the window, needing to catch a glimpse of the black bird, wondering if it had been the one I saw the night of the attack—not that I would've been able to identify the crow from other birds. I stopped listening to Satella as she talked about her last patient.

I stood, the sudden urge to go outside taking over. "I have to go."

"Where?" Satella asked, but I barely heard her as I flew out of the room.

The air was warm against my skin. It was one of the warmest days since I had arrived at Ethlow. I kept my eyes focused on the sky, looking for the obnoxious crow, but it had settled the moment I stepped outside. Then a caw echoed from the trees. I moved, following it the best I could. Every time I lost sight of it, it made a noise, leading me right to it.

The crow landed on the roof of the greenhouse. I had been too caught up with following it to realize where it was taking me, but now that the building was right in front of me, I couldn't get my feet to move. It'd only take a couple of steps to enter, to see if Zathrian was inside, waiting for me to show up.

I took a step back, fear wrapping itself around my heart. If I stepped through the door and Zathrian wasn't waiting for me, I wasn't sure I could handle it.

The crow cawed, and it sounded like it said, *Coward.*

I glared at the bird. "Don't act like you know everything. You're a bird."

Caw! Rude.

I blinked several times. I was going crazy. Arguing with a bird was a new low.

"Fine," I muttered. I took a step forward, and my heart raced faster the closer I got.

The door to the greenhouse was fixed. The glass looked like it was new, and it didn't creak as I opened it. The inside took my breath away. It looked nothing like it had before. The debris and dead plants had been cleared away. The patches of broken glass were fixed. The sun beat down through the glass, creating a warm and humid environment. The tables were cleared off, empty pots replacing the mess. It was as if the greenhouse had been completely reset, and it was waiting for my touch to bring it back to life.

Other than the trees, there was one other plant left alive. I moved towards a thick, green vine that had been working its way up the glass. The leaves were deep green and happy. I stepped closer and ran my fingers over the plant. It had been dead the last time I came to the greenhouse. I was sure it had no life left in its body when I touched it.

Did I do that?

I hadn't thought about my magic much since the library incident. I hadn't gone back—especially after I heard Tareen was livid at the destruction she had discovered after leaving me alone. I hadn't wanted to face her, not when I was trying to figure out how to piece back together my broken heart.

I couldn't think of any other explanation for the thriving plant other than magic. Even if the vine hadn't been dead, it would've been impossible for it to grow that much in such a short amount of time.

"I was told you would show up eventually."

I spun around, but the demon I had hoped to see wasn't there. Instead, Viridian stood at the door, holding a small white box tied with a red ribbon.

"Are you here to kick me out of Ethlow?" I figured it was only a matter of time for the master of the house to punish me for breaking the third rule and causing him problems.

He tilted his head to the side, making his neck crack. He returned to his normal position before speaking. "I thought about the different ways I could punish you. I quickly decided against sending you back out into the world. You can't even stay out of trouble here. You'd be dead in a week on your own."

"That's not true," I snapped. I wasn't skilled, but I had managed the trip to Ethlow. If I was kicked out, I was sure I'd figure out *something*.

"Right." The word was drawn out and filled with disbelief. "My personal favorite punishment is cutting off a finger and toe from each limb, making you choose which digit." I cringed at the suggestion, quickly reminded of his brutality. "But then I decided that wouldn't do. Your work would become even more sloppy and inefficient. Malse would throw a fit if I rendered one of her seamstresses useless." He dropped the hand that had been tucked behind his back a moment prior. He curled his fingers, emphasizing the long, black nails that had pierced my neck, his white gloves nowhere to be seen. "In the end, I decided you faced enough punishment at the hands of King Jathral. Besides, any pain to you would also cause the young sire pain."

Viridian was careful with his words. He didn't say or do anything he didn't want anyone to know about. He intentionally let it slip that hurting me would hurt Zathrian—who he cared about. That also meant the argument in front of Satella's room was intentional. Viridian *wanted* me to hear Zathrian's plea to see me. The master of the house wanted me to know Zathrian cared for me, but I didn't understand why.

"You care deeply for Zathrian," I said.

Viridian didn't show a physical response. "I am the master of the house. It is my responsibility to make sure Ethlow runs smoothly. That cannot happen if the sire is distressed. That is all."

Viridian was cold and calculating enough that it would've been easy for me to believe him. Only I didn't believe he was simply the master of the house. He was a powerful demon, one that could subdue two of the strongest known demons with words alone. He was more than he was letting on, but I knew he wouldn't tell me the truth unless he wanted me to know.

"It was against the rules to see Zathrian, and I understand why now. It only hurt both of us. I should've listened to your warnings." It hurt to say that out loud. I craved to see Zathrian again. It wasn't just the physical aspect—even though that was incredible. I ached to be near him, to see him smile, to hear him laugh.

"You're right. You should've listened. If you had, we wouldn't be in this situation."

"I'll stay away from him." I didn't want to, but I was done being a foolish girl. I wanted a quiet life, not one where demons attacked me in libraries. I knew I could have a happy life now that Satella and Aukina were my friends. I grew up being told I'd die alone as a spinster if I didn't lose weight. Things were different. As long as I had people by my side who cared about me, I'd be okay. I didn't need to find a life partner.

Viridian walked over to the rows of tables. He placed the small box on top of the metal surface. He clasped his hands behind his back before looking at me. "I have come to understand recently that some rules should be treated more as... guidelines. Do with that as you will." The demon walked away, but he paused at the door. He looked over his shoulder, his eyes flashing black. "If you intentionally hurt him, I won't hesitate to kill you."

Then he was gone.

I couldn't move. Viridian's threat should have terrified me, but it didn't sound like a threat. It sounded like his blessing.

I looked at the little box the demon left behind. I approached it slowly, unsure of what it was. I opened the lid and gasped, nearly dropping it. Sitting on top of a small cushion, there was a red seed close to the size of a walnut. The shape resembled a human heart. I had only seen drawings of it, but I instantly knew what it was. The seed of a bleeding heart lily.

There was only one being who I had told about my dream of the elusive flower. Not even Aukina or Satella knew my passion for the rare flower. There was only one being who could've known what that kind of gift would mean to me. Underneath the seed, there was a folded note. I carefully set the box and the seed on the table before unfolding the small piece of paper.

You are special, which is how I know you will make this bleeding heart lily bloom, like you made my heart bloom again when I thought it was impossible.

Tears spilled onto the paper, and my hands shook. I had spent days telling myself things between Zathrian and I were over, but it had been a fool's errand. Even if being with him meant facing dangerous demons, I didn't care. I could create a simple, happy life without a lover, but I didn't want that kind of life. I wanted love and passion.

I wanted Zathrian.

Chapter 19

I had never run that fast in my entire life. By the time I made it to the top of the stairs, I had to stop to catch my breath. It felt like my heart was going to burst, either from the need to see Zathrian to confirm I wasn't making up false interpretations from Viridian's words or from running faster than my body was capable of.

Before I could breathe properly, I continued running until I stood in front of the demon king's door. I lifted my hand to knock, but before my hand hit the door, I froze. Zathrian wanted me. He wouldn't clean up the greenhouse and find me a seed of the bleeding heart lily if he didn't care.

Except I thought my family wanted me. I thought they loved me, and they threw me away like an old rag.

I closed my eyes and rapped my knuckles against the wood. Because my family didn't love me the way I loved them, it didn't mean I was destined to be alone and unloved for the rest of my life. Aukina and Satella showed me that.

The door creaked open, and I opened my mouth, prepared to tell Zathrian thank you, but he wasn't alone. My mouth gaped open as a young woman, probably around eighteen, measured his torso, running her fingers over his sides, measuring the length between his wings. A twinge rippled through my chest.

A young man who looked similar to the girl stared at me. "Can we help you?" he asked.

I closed my mouth, not wanting to look like a complete idiot. I hadn't thought for one second that Zathrian would be anything other than alone. It was against the rules to fraternize with the demon king.

I took a step back. "I'm sorry. I'll come back later."

Zathrian snapped his head, the sound of my voice bringing his attention to me. The young man started to close the door, but Zathrian lifted his hand. "No." The word made the two in his room flinch. The demon king cleared his throat before speaking again at a regular volume. "We'll continue this later. Please excuse us."

The woman nodded her head and stepped off her little stool. The young man helped her collect her belongings. I stepped to the side, giving them plenty of space to leave. I didn't enter the room, even as their footsteps faded.

"I didn't mean to interrupt," I said.

Zathrian hadn't moved from his spot, either. He looked at me, hardly breathing. "I wasn't sure I'd ever see you again. I didn't think you'd..." His voice fell off, and he took a strained breath. He was hurting, like I was.

Knowing that, gave me the courage I needed to step into his room. I closed the door behind me, but I faced the door, afraid to look him in the eyes as I spoke. "I thought it was best that we didn't see each other anymore. I understand why you said it was dangerous to be with you now."

"I wanted to kill Jathral for touching you. If I had known he would've found you in the library, I would've assigned guards to you. I should've protected you."

"I was your dirty little secret. If you had done any of that, everyone would've known that something was going on between us." I huffed, shaking my head. "I guess it doesn't matter anymore."

Zathrian's footsteps were barely audible as he approached, but I was tuned into his every movement. His heat wrapped around my spine, but he didn't touch me. I ached for him to reach out and run his fingers through my hair again. I wanted to wrap my arms around his neck and pull him into a kiss, but I couldn't. Not yet.

"You were never just a dirty little secret to me." He lifted his hand, but he dropped it again, as if thinking better of his actions.

I spun around and pressed my back against the door, pinning my hands behind me. I didn't trust myself not to touch him. The moment our skin made contact, I wouldn't be able to think clearly. I lifted my chin, looking up at the demon king. He held himself like royalty, strong and unyielding. Only his eyes were hollow, as if a deep loneliness threatened to take over him.

"Tell me what happened to Leira." I hated asking the question. I didn't want to bring up old pain for Zathrian, but if I was going to give in to my heart again, I had to know the truth.

Zathrian held my eyes as he spoke. He wasn't going to hide from his past. "We fell in love accidentally, and she died because of it."

THE DEMON KING'S PET

"How?" I could barely speak the word. The demon king's answer would determine the path I'd take to my future.

"When demons take a lover, it is common for us to mark them, to let other demons know they are not to touch what belongs to another. Leira and I were in love. We spent every second of our free time together. I asked her how she felt about the mark, and she told me to do it immediately. She loved the idea of everyone knowing who she belonged to, so I marked her. I thought it would make her safe." There was so much guilt in his last words that I almost told him to stop. I didn't want to make him relive such a painful memory.

But I had to know.

"With that mark, everyone knew who claimed her. As demon king, I have many enemies, enemies that suddenly knew my weakness. They used her against me, and I was too late. I failed to protect her." He finally looked away from me, curling his fingers into fists. "The counsel of demons learned about the incident, and they punished me for it. I am a demon king. If I cannot keep my own residents safe, then I don't deserve to claim anyone as my own."

"Is that why the rule to stay away from you was created?" I asked.

"Yes and no. The council didn't make the rule, but Viridian thought it was the best way to keep the residents at Ethlow safe. The counsel forbade me to mark anyone as my own. Viridian made it so that I couldn't get close enough to someone to fall for them."

"That's horrible. You've been alone all of this time because of a mistake that wasn't even your fault?" Pressure built in my chest as anger pulsed through my veins. I didn't know who to direct that anger towards.

"Viridian's first priority is to protect me from enemies. His second is to protect the residents of Ethlow. When he suggested the rule, I didn't hesitate to agree to it. I deserved to be alone for not protecting Leira. She had come here for a new life, and instead, she lost her life because of me."

I reached up and touched Zathrian's chest, unable to hold back any longer. "It's not your fault."

Zathrian pulled away from me. "But it is. I wasn't the one who put a blade through her heart, but I promised to keep her safe after announcing to the world that she was precious to me. That is why I don't deserve to mark anyone. I don't deserve to fall in love. I don't deserve you."

I felt the two of us standing on a thin strip of land with cliffs on either side of us. One wrong step, and we'd tumble into the ravine, forever losing each other. I had spent days trying to convince myself that it was for the best, but it had been a lie.

I stepped forward and grabbed Zathrian's hand. He tried to pull away, but I tightened my grip, and he stopped fighting. "Everyone deserves to be loved, including you. If anything, I'm the one who doesn't deserve you. I have accomplished nothing in my life, except for being too much of a burden that my family tossed me onto the streets without a care. I'm mediocre at sewing. The food I cook is questionably edible, and I can't lose weight for the life of me. I couldn't tell that I had magic. Yet, you never saw those things. You touched me like you thought I was beautiful. You made me feel safe and wanted."

"I also got you attacked. Jathral only attacked you because he scented me on you."

My throat tightened as a flash of fear rang through my body. The things Jathral had said scared me, but what scared me more was losing Zathrian. I lifted onto my toes and cupped his face. I needed Zathrian to hear the words I was about to say, because if the guilt continued to eat away at him, I'd lose him forever. "That was *not* your fault. Jathral is the only one responsible for his actions. You saved me from him."

"I can't promise others won't come after you," he said. His eyes turned glassy, his emotions building behind his precious, golden eyes.

"Then we'll face them together, because I would rather risk getting attacked than spend the rest of my life missing you."

"I... I can't mark you." His walls were breaking down.

"I don't care. As long as I'm with you, then I don't care." My heart refused to slow down. I was close to getting Zathrian's barriers to collapse. He wanted this as much as me, but he was also scared.

"What about the rules?" He was grasping at straws.

"Someone once told me that some rules are meant to be treated more like guidelines." I slid my hands down to his chest, feeling the racing of both his hearts. "You fixed the greenhouse for me and found the seed of a bleeding heart lily. If you think I'm going to let you go that easily, you're crazy."

Zathrian leaned forward, pressing his forehead against mine. "Those were meant as a goodbye. I wanted to make sure you could be happy and live a good life here."

"As long as I have you, I will. I'm not going to lie and say I'm not scared of what will happen, but I know I'm terrified about finding out what a life without you is like. So I'd rather be scared together."

Zathrian slid his fingers into my hair and pulled me closer, closing the gap between our mouths. The moment our lips touched, a surge ran through my body, and I knew Zathrian was the right choice. There was no going back to a simple life. "Then let's be scared together."

Chapter
20

Z athrian adjusted his suit again. He was nervous, but it was cute. He was the demon king, feared by many, but he was nervous to go see the residents of Ethlow.

"Wasn't this your idea?" I asked, watching him from the bed.

He looked at me through the mirror. "I don't want to hide anymore. I want to be an active presence in Ethlow."

"Then what are you worried about?" I rolled onto my back and let my head fall off the edge. I watched him upside down, tugging at my dress. I didn't wear them often since they weren't ideal for gardening, but Aukina had insisted I dress up for the occasion.

"What if they hate me?" He turned away from the mirror, and his eyes immediately went to my thighs. Blood rushed to my face from a combination of dangling upside down and excitement.

"You can't control what others think of you. Some people are going to hate you simply for being a demon. Others will hate you because you're the king."

"Thanks," he muttered.

"What I'm trying to say is people are going to hate you for reasons you can't control. Show the people of Ethlow who you are, and the rest will fall into place." I stretched my arms above my head and let out a long groan. I hadn't had enough sleep in weeks for reasons I couldn't complain about. My body wanted to protest being awake. When I opened my eyes, Zathrian was leaning over, looking at me.

"What if your friends don't like me?" The close proximity of his face made my thighs squeeze together. I wondered if I'd ever be able to look at the demon king without thinking dirty thoughts.

"They will love you. They will tease you—especially Satella—but it's out of love." Satella and Aukina had been begging to meet Zathrian for weeks, but Zathrian had insisted on waiting until things with Jathral had settled, wanting to make sure the other demon king didn't try to cause more issues.

"We'll see about that." He kissed my lips lightly, making my eyes flutter shut.

"How much time do we have?" I asked as he pulled away.

His deep chuckle reverberated in my chest. "Not enough time for what you're thinking."

I pushed myself to a sitting position before rolling onto my knees. "I wasn't thinking anything like *that*."

Zathrian pressed his hands onto the bed, hovering only a few inches away from my face. "Are you sure about that?" His tail slid up my thigh, easily moving between my legs. My legs spread automatically, giving him better access. He rubbed his tail over my underwear, making me moan. "That's what I thought." He chuckled again.

My eyes snapped open, and I pursed my lips. I was about to complain about him teasing me, but he pushed my underwear to the side, dipping his tail through my folds. A moan replaced my complaint, especially as he flicked my little bundle of nerves. "Zathrian," I whispered.

He kissed my lips and hummed, "Yes?"

"Don't stop." It was an order, one with a threat behind it. If he stopped after getting me riled up, he would face serious consequences.

Zathrian climbed on top of me as I lay down, never pulling his tail out of me. His hands pressed into the bed next to me as he brushed his nose against mine before his mouth found mine. His tail pushed into my entrance as his tongue slipped past my lips. I parted my mouth, eagerly taking him in.

I ran my fingers through his hair. When I wrapped my hands around his horns, he groaned at the sensation.

"Do you have any idea what you do to me when you touch me like that?" he muttered, barely breaking from the kiss.

"Maybe." I moved my hands up and down, eliciting another moan from him.

"You taunt me, my pet," he growled lowly. "Better be careful. You may not be able to handle the consequences."

"I can handle anything as long as you're with me." I pulled Zathrian closer and kissed him deeply. His tongue tangled with mine as he dragged his hand down my side, softly caressing me.

I arched into his touch, but then he wiggled his fingers, tickling my side. I squealed and squirmed beneath him. He grabbed my hands with one of his, pinning me to the bed as he continued to assault my side. His laugh was like an evil chuckle as he took pleasure in the way I was defenseless against him.

"No," I cried out, but he was too strong for me.

Zathrian stopped, smirking down at me. "I thought you could handle anything," he taunted.

I scrunched my nose, not wanting to admit I was wrong. "You broke the rules."

"What rules?"

"The rules that say you can't tickle me during intimacy."

He brushed his nose against mine. "Some rules are meant to be treated more like guidelines."

I opened my mouth to argue against the words I had said to him recently, but his mouth captured mine, preventing any arguments from escaping. When he parted, both of us were silent as we gazed into each other's eyes. My chest warmed, and I wondered if that was what it felt like to feel truly happy.

"Zathrian?"

"Yes?" he hummed.

"I want you."

Desire danced in his eyes. "You don't have to tell me twice."

With his tail, he pulled down my underwear. He released my hands, and pulled his pants down, freeing his cock. He lifted my legs up, guiding himself to my entrance. Before he pushed in, he kissed me, taking his time and making sure I was ready for him. I hooked my leg around his, ready for all of him to be inside of me. He moved forward, thrusting into me. I moaned as he stretched me out, loving every second of it.

He kissed me slowly as he moved back and forth, taking his time, despite the time restraint we had. I didn't complain. I could stay with him in bed all day if our obligations didn't pull us away. Slowly, he picked up his pace. He pulled my thigh higher, changing the angle he thrusted into me and hitting the spot that made my eyes roll backwards.

Sensing the build up in my core, Zathrian flicked his tail over my sensitive bundle of nerves. The dam collapsed, and pure ecstasy ran through my veins. He found his own high before collapsing next to me. He pulled me into his chest as we caught our breaths, neither of us wanting to speak and ruin the moment.

My cheeks were flushed as I walked through the trees hand-in-hand with Zathrian. We were never going to hide our relationship again, and that felt better than I had ever imagined. Many residents of Ethlow waited for us at the greenhouse. I was certain the majority of the people were there because they wanted to see Zathrian. He had been an elusive figure for decades. Many of the current residents had never seen him.

Others wanted to confirm the rumors about us dating. Most of the beings weren't here to see the newly opened greenhouse, but that was fine with me. The people I cared about most were there for me.

Satella and Aukina waved their hands as I approached. Satella stood in the sun, taking in the sunlight with her pale skin. Aukina stuck to the shade of a tree, even though her skin was better built for the sun.

As Zathrian and I approached, the crowd quieted down. I scanned the bodies for any sign of Viridian. I hadn't seen him since he found me in the greenhouse weeks ago, but evidence of his work was all over the estate. I wondered if he'd show up today. Part of me worried I had misinterpreted his words, and he'd show up, forbidding Zathrian and I to continue seeing each other.

Viridian wasn't there, but Malse was. I no longer worked as a seamstress. Zathrian had decided my work with the greenhouse was sufficient, since it'd provide essential supplies to Ethlow. It allowed me to spend all of my free time in the glass building, preparing for today.

I hesitated to move forward. I was excited to show the residents of Ethlow what I had created, but I wasn't prepared to speak in front of a crowd. Zathrian gently pushed my back, encouraging me to step forward and be proud of my work. I let go of his hand and walked to the door of the greenhouse alone. I had worked hard and created something special. I wanted to be proud of that, instead of hiding.

"Many of you may not know me," I said. Satella motioned her hands upward, encouraging me to speak louder. I cleared my throat and summoned as much gusto as I could manage. "I've been working on this place for a while now, and it's finally ready to share with you all. The greenhouse is a resource for Ethlow, and I want it to be a place where everyone who wants to can use it. We will have a section dedicated to growing food for the kitchen and growing medicinal plants, but there are areas where people can tend to their own plants, if they desire. All requests for space should be sent to me for approval. I'm also open to teaching anyone who wishes to learn to garden."

Satella clapped her hands, the only one who cheered for my little speech. I looked at Zathrian, and he gave me a nod of encouragement. Joy bloomed in my chest. It felt as if everything in my life was finally falling into place. I had friends and a place where I could garden in peace. And then there was Zathrian. I knew being with one of the five demon kings wasn't going to be easy. Trouble would come to us, but for now, I was happy.

"If you all will follow me, I'd like to show you something special." I opened the door and led the crowd inside.

In the center of the room, there was a small table with a cloth covering what was beneath. I waited for everyone to settle, and then I pulled it off, revealing a fully bloomed bleeding heart lily. Gasps and murmurs echoed around the room from those who recognized the flower. Those who didn't know were quickly informed by others.

"This is a bleeding heart lily, grown by me." And my new magic. "It is rare, especially on the continent, but I plan on growing a whole section of these flowers, so that everyone at Ethlow can enjoy their beauty. If anyone has questions about the flower or the greenhouse, feel free to approach me. Thank you all for coming."

The crowd dispersed, half of them leaving the building—those were the beings who didn't care about the greenhouse to begin with—and half staying to explore the greenhouse. Satella and Aukina ran up to me first.

Aukina took both of my hands. "This is what you have been keeping a secret? It's incredible. I haven't seen a bleeding heart lily since... since I was back home." Tears bubbled in her eyes as lost memories came back to her. I didn't know much about her past, other than she had felt unwanted both on land and in the sea.

"I wanted to surprise you," I said. I wasn't sure if the flower would remind Aukina of home, but her home island was one of the few places the flower was known to thrive.

"Surprise us, you did," Satella said. Her gaze shifted to Zathrian who was walking over to us. "Although I'm not surprised you were late with him sharing your bed."

My cheeks heated, knowing Satella saw right through us. She probably guessed the reason we were late the moment she saw my flushed cheeks.

Zathrian cleared his throat, likely overhearing the conversation. I moved over to him, wrapping my arms around him, not caring who saw me. "Hi," I whispered, looking up at the demon king. He smiled as he looked down at me. His eyes were lighter than they had been since I met him, as if a heavy burden had been lifted off his chest.

"Hi." He leaned down and kissed my forehead.

"Ugh. You two are stupid cute," Satella said as Aukina gushed at the interaction.

"I wish I could find that kind of love," Aukina added.

I bit my lower lip. I wasn't used to this much attention, and Zathrian and I hadn't confessed feelings like that to each other. Everything had felt too new, and I didn't want to ruin anything because of words.

"You will," I said, trying not to let my conflicted emotions form my facial expressions.

"You should confess to that merchant you've been eying," Satella said.

Aukina's face turned bright red. "I don't know what you're talking about. I should get back to the kitchen."

Satella gave a knowing smile. "I should return to work as well. Have fun you two." She waved at us as she followed the embarrassed mermaid out of the greenhouse.

"You look happy," Zathrian whispered in my ear, making me realize I hadn't stopped smiling.

"I am," I said. I watched the various residents of Ethlow gush over the different plants, especially when they went up to the bleeding heart lily to get a better look. I had created something special, something others admired. It felt good to be recognized for my work.

"Good," he said. He twisted his finger around a strand of my hair. "I do, by the way."

I looked up at him, confused. "You do what?"

His smile brightened, making him look nothing like what I had expected from a demon. "I love you."

My heart fluttered in my chest and all thoughts left my head. I hadn't expected him to say those words, not when anyone could overhear us.

"I love you, too." The words were easier to say than I had expected. I had never confessed to anyone like that before, but with Zathrian, it was natural.

His smile only grew brighter. He gently guided my head to his, kissing me as if no one was watching. Any doubt I once had about pursuing more with a demon king disappeared. I was happy in a way I thought could only happen in fantasies, and I was excited about what the future held for me and for my life at Ethlow.

As Zathrian pulled away, I caught sight of the glowing teal eyes that had greeted me my first day at Ethlow. Viridian stood near the door with his hands clasped behind his back. As our eyes met, he gave a single curt nod, as if he was giving his blessing to the union between Zathrian and me. I nodded back, hoping he knew what I was trying to tell him. I planned to take care of Zathrian as if he was my own heart.

"What are you looking at?" Zathrian asked.

I looked at him and then back at Viridian, only the master of the house was gone. "Nothing," I said. I intertwined my fingers with his. "I want to show you the bleeding heart lily up close. Come on."

The residents of Ethlow stopped what they were doing to look at us, and I held my head high, proud of who I was for the first time in my life.

WANT TO STAY CONNECTED?

Be the first to learn about new releases, receive bonus scenes, receive ARC opportunities, and learn more about Eri Everland by subscribing to her newsletter here.

TikTok: @eri.everland.author

Instagram: @eri.everland.author

Newsletter: subscribe@erieverland.com

Also by Eri Everland
AKA Ever Eri

The Demons of Kinzlea

The Demon King's Pet
The Demon King's Cook
The Demon King's Healer
The Demon King's Librarian
The Demon King's Teacher
The Demon King's Assassin

The Demons of Valenmae

The Demon Queen's Rise
The Infernal Dagger (Novella)
The Demon Queen's Fall
The Demon Queen's Wrath

The Unfortunate Fate of Mates

Available on the Dreame App:

The Four Beta Brothers

The Stolen Wolf Princess

The Long Lost Luna

The Unwanted Wolf

The Blood Moon Twins

AUTHOR'S NOTE

Thank you so much for taking time to read my book! If you've made it this far, I would greatly appreciate it if you took the time to leave a review on Amazon/Goodreads. As an indie author, reviews are essential for gaining more visibility. All reviews are appreciated! If you ever have any questions, concerns, or general comments, please feel free to reach out to me directly at eri@evereriauthor.com.

For more, check out evereriauthor.com.

ACKNOWLEDGEMENTS

To my friends who have been there for me at my worst and at my best. Your support has made it possible to believe in myself enough to take this journey.

For Kelly who suffers through my most raw writing.

For Lauren who has listened to me talk about countless story ideas.

For Sam who brainstorms monsters with me.

For Amanda and the inspiration you have given me on our coffee dates.

For friendship bracelets, relentless teasing, healing hugs, and late night laughter.

www.ingramcontent.com/pod-product-compliance
Lightning Source LLC
Chambersburg PA
CBHW022114170626
46808CB00002B/728